She looked at Pax again ... her fingers itched to stroke and the dark eyes she could drown in if she wasn't careful.

At the tattooed letters inked below his elegant collarbone. She could make out the second word now, so the phrase began with *Down these*, but the rest of whatever it said disappeared beneath the fabric of his shirt—as did the broad shoulders straining against the garment. At the full mouth, half curled into a flirty smile, which she suddenly wanted to stand up on tiptoe to kiss.

She had to curl her fingers into fists at her sides to keep from touching him. Because in that moment, all she wanted to do was touch Pax. And kiss Pax. And wake up in the morning beside Pax. It had just been so long since she had shared any kind of closeness with anyone. And now a man who looked like a paladin from one of her favorite novels, a man filled with warmth and wit and good will, a man who was so much—dayum—so much sexier than any guy she had ever encountered...

Dear Reader,

I came of age in the '60s and '70s, when the women's movement was in full swing. As an adolescent, I was so excited about potential equality that I even canceled my subscription to *Cat Fancy* so I could use my allowance for *Ms.* instead. Women were on a roll!

Then, suddenly, we weren't. By now women were supposed to be running the world alongside men as equal partners. But instead of being viewed as equal partners, women are too often viewed as prey.

Emma Brown is just such a woman. The entire online manosphere is gunning for her after she had the temerity to publicly point out—rightfully so—that their toxic masculinity guru isn't exactly the sharpest knife in the drawer. The cyber backlash has been so bad, she's had to go underground and on the run, and she has no idea whom she can trust. Certainly no one with a Y chromosome.

Then she meets Pax Lightfoot, Y chromosome. His masculinity doesn't *seem* toxic. In fact, his masculinity looks pretty dang good from where she's standing. And no, of course it's not all men. But when there's an angry torch-bearing mob of them breathing down your neck, it sure feels like it. What's an internet pariah to do?

Emma's story has been one of my favorites to write. I hope you enjoy reading it, too.

Stay fierce!

Elizabeth

KEEPING HER SECRET

ELIZABETH BEVARLY

SPECIAL EDITION

Harlequin®
SPECIAL
EDITION™

Recycling programs
for this product may
not exist in your area.

ISBN-13: 978-1-335-40219-6

Keeping Her Secret

Copyright © 2025 by Elizabeth Bevarly

For questions and comments about the quality of this book, please contact us at CustomerService@Harlequin.com.

TM and ® are trademarks of Harlequin Enterprises ULC.

Harlequin Enterprises ULC
22 Adelaide St. West, 41st Floor
Toronto, Ontario M5H 4E3, Canada
www.Harlequin.com

Printed in Lithuania

MIX
Paper | Supporting
responsible forestry
FSC® C021394

Elizabeth Bevarly is the *New York Times* and *USA TODAY* bestselling author of more than eighty books. She has called home such exotic places as Puerto Rico and New Jersey but now lives outside her hometown of Louisville, Kentucky, with her husband and cat. When she's not writing or reading, she enjoys cooking, tending her kitchen garden and feeding the local wildlife. Visit her at elizabethbevarly.com for news and lots of fun stuff.

For every woman who has ever
felt unsafe around a man.
In other words, all of us.
Stay fierce.

Chapter One

Emma Brown gazed out the tiny window of her tiny third-floor room in the massive Gilded Age mansion she called home—for now—and tried to relax. Which was something she hadn't been able to do for too long. She didn't care if the room and the window were tiny. The view beyond them was nothing short of spectacular. She'd never been to Upstate New York, and she'd had no idea how gorgeous it was. Cayuga Lake's deep sapphire waters sparkled under a golden sun as rolling green hills fell away on the other side. Between them, on the opposite shore, was a small Finger Lakes village much like the one on this side, its mottled rooftops and staggered chimneys looking like something from a Dickens novel.

Two blue herons picked their way slowly along the shoreline as a family of mallards swam past them. She pushed the two French windows open wider to invite in a warm, early June breeze that ruffled her bangs and the sandy hair dancing around her shoulders. Then she closed her eyes and inhaled the first breath of freedom she'd taken in nine months. Freedom smelled very nice indeed—a mix of pine and damp earth and wild bergamot, so different from the city smells of dumpster and sewer and bus exhaust that had been her companions for too long.

Oh, yes. She would definitely breathe easier here in the little village of Sudbury. No bursts of car alarms to interrupt her sleep. No picking through dumpsters for past-sell-by goods tossed behind the grocery stores. No shivering under flimsy overhangs in drenched clothing to wait for the storms to pass. No hunger. No terror. No nightmares.

And no death threats. Yeah, that was a definite bonus. This place would do nicely. At least for a little while.

"What do you think?" the woman standing in the doorway behind her asked. "I know it's not a lot, but it's a far cry from the storage room it was when Bennett and I moved in last fall—trust me."

With much reluctance, Emma turned her back on the scene out the window to study the room instead. Haven Moreau, one of her two new employers, looked as if she feared Emma would renege on her acceptance of the position of housekeeper at the soon-to-be-open bed-and-breakfast now that she'd seen her lodging. She didn't look much older than Emma, nor was she dressed the way most employers usually dressed. Her pale blond hair was gathered into a ponytail from which half of it was spilling out, her jeans were torn at both knees in a way that didn't look as if it had been done for the sake of fashion, and her oversize T-shirt bore the name of a place called Vinnie's House of Hammers.

Of course, Haven had been outside doing something to the window shutters with a power tool of some kind when Emma arrived, so these were probably her usual work clothes. The super casual attire, however, made Emma feel even more at home here. Her other employer was Haven's fiancé, Bennett Haddon, whom Emma had yet to meet. But if he was even half as easygoing and welcoming as Haven was, Emma would be fine.

She drove her gaze around the room one more time. The twelve-by-twelve space was crowded with a wrought-iron twin bed, bird's-eye maple dresser and armoire, and a slipper chair upholstered in faded, plum-colored moiré. A worn hooked wool rug spattered with cabbage roses spanned much of the hardwood floor.

It was a far cry from the open-plan Seattle condo filled with ultra-sleek, very beige modern furniture in the glass-and-chrome high-rise she had called home this time last summer. The one she had almost certainly lost to foreclosure by now. Lost, too, she was sure, were all the possessions she'd had to leave behind. The fully loaded state-of-the-art twenty-seven-inch iMac Pro desktop with which she'd made her living. The cosmetics case filled with eyeliners and contouring brushes and more Dior lipsticks than you could shake a stick at—mattes *and* frosteds. The Pokémon-card collection she'd so meticulously curated for years. The Pandora bracelet to which she had been adding charms for nearly a decade—every time she'd had some kind of success, large or small, to commemorate, since com-memorations of anything had been glaringly absent from her childhood.

Gone. All of it. And so much more. Because of one stupid, minutes-long lapse in judgment. When would she learn to keep her mouth shut? She was beginning to think she was never going to get her life back. Never going to get herself back. That said, however—

"It's perfect," Emma assured her new boss. "I love it."

And she was surprised to realize she was being more honest in that moment than she'd ever been in her life.

Haven smiled in clear relief. "For now, the bathroom at the end of the hall is all yours, but we'll eventually be hiring a full-time concierge and a full-time grounds-keeper who will have the other two bedrooms up here, and then you'll have to share that bathroom with them."

A tiny bedroom and shared bathroom would be a luxury compared to what Emma had been having to do since last September. Sleeping in secluded city alleys in the worst of times, hiding out in libraries and shopping malls until they closed in the best. Sneaking into athletic clubs whenever she could to shower, picking through the previously mentioned dumpsters to find something, anything, to eat. Eventually, she'd been able to take odd jobs here and there that paid in cash, but even with those, there had never been enough to afford an actual hotel or restaurant—not even the cut-rate kind. Whatever she'd had to do to find a relatively safe place to sleep and reasonably decent food to eat, Emma had done it. And those had been the *good* days. Life on the run had been worse than she could have ever imagined. This little room in the middle of nowhere was a palace compared to some of the places she'd been living for the past nine months.

"That's totally fine," she said. "Truly. I've lived in worse conditions."

Understatement of the century.

"Well, I'm sorry to hear that," Haven said. "But I'm very happy you'll be working with me and Bennett to bring Summerlight back to life." With a bright smile, she added, "We're almost there. Opening in a little over five months! I can hardly believe it. You should have seen this place when we moved in." She shuddered for dramatic effect. "Bennett and I didn't exactly see eye to eye on plans for the place at first, so it took some time to get it going. But once we finally figured things out—" Here, she smiled in a way that suggested it wasn't just the house she and her husband-to-be had needed to come to deal with "—well, everything just sort of fell into place after that. Of course, it made a mess when it fell, but…" She shrugged. "Anyway, we've come a long way. You're actually our first official hire. Yay you."

Yay me, Emma echoed to herself with a smile of her own. She hadn't had much to celebrate for the past year. Or, you know, anything to celebrate. She'd take whatever festivity she could get.

She'd found out about the job opening here the old-fashioned way—through the want ads in a weekly newspaper. She didn't dare go online these days any more than she had to. Although she was probably safe enough at this point from being ID'd, she'd been traumatized enough at the beginning to never want to go online again. Funny for someone who'd built a very successful business by spending pretty much her whole life online. These days she only ventured onto the internet to make very quick, very perfunctory looks around, and only on public computers. She'd had to learn to zig and zag her way from the West Coast to the East the way people had traveled a hundred years ago—with paper maps and public transportation. There had been times when Emma felt like she'd fallen back in time to the Great Depression, the way she'd had to pick up odd jobs here and there to earn enough money to make it to the next place, wherever that place ended up being.

Because there had always had to be another place after she left Seattle. Early on, it had been because someone told her she looked *so* familiar for some reason. A couple of times, it had been because someone told her flat out that she looked just like that girl everyone was looking for online. After those incidents, Emma had simply been too scared to stick around in one place for very long. So as soon as she earned a few bucks, off she would go again, to wherever she could afford a bus ticket. From Seattle to Butte. From Butte to Bismarck. From Bismarck to St. Cloud. Then south after winter set in to avoid the bitter cold. Fort Smith. Tupelo. Pensacola. Waycross. But still there had been occasions when she was recognized, and it was all she could do to escape before someone took a photo of her the way she looked now to post online and make finding her even easier.

On and on she had traveled, avoiding all the larger cities, lighting for as long as it took to get somewhere else. With any luck, she could call home this little room through next spring. The heat on her that had been so scorching nine months ago had ebbed to a glow-ing ember by now, but it could flicker back to a raging inferno if she wasn't careful. Even so, she felt safe enough by now to spend more than a month in one place. As long as she remained vigilant. And as long as she stayed offline.

"I'm glad to be here," she told Haven.

Another understatement of the century.

"Well, I'll leave you to get settled," her employer told her.

Yeah, that ought to take about fifteen minutes. She'd barely made it out of her condo with the clothes on her back last fall. On the upside, she'd had the foresight to pack a grab-and-go bag after the first time her front door got kicked in. On the downside, all she'd put in it were a couple of T-shirts, a few pairs of underwear and some jeans. She'd figured at the time that if she *did* have to vacate the premises again—which she hadn't thought was likely after having a locksmith install a half dozen new locks and a new reinforced security door—she wouldn't have to be gone for long. Hah. Since then, she'd managed to collect a couple of peasanty skirts, a button-up shirt, a sweater, some sandals and a five-pack of underwear. Along with the jeans, black T-shirt and hiking boots she wore now, that was the entirety of Emma's wardrobe these days. A far cry from the closet full of punk and goth thrift finds she'd also had to leave behind.

"If you need anything," Haven added, "let me know. I'll work out your schedule this evening, if you don't mind starting tomorrow."

"Tomorrow would be great," Emma assured her. The

sooner she began collecting a paycheck, the better. Not that the paychecks here at Summerlight would be anything to write home about, since her room and board were included as a big part of her employment package. But that was fine with her. She was in a beautiful place. A quiet place. A safe place. A place where she wouldn't awaken every morning to the fear of whether or not someone was going to recognize her today and how she was going to find enough to eat and where she would be sleeping once night fell again.

It really had been a crappy nine months.

Haven smiled again. "Perfect." She gestured toward the dresser in the corner. "I left a folder for you about Summerlight's history—which is actually pretty interesting, filled with larger-than-life characters and wild misunderstandings and generations-long family feuds—and our plans for opening the weekend before Thanksgiving. Your job description is in there, too, but it's all pretty basic. Tomorrow morning, after breakfast, we can go over all the paperwork. Welcome to Sudbury," she added. "You're going to love it here—I promise."

Even knowing she would be filling out that paperwork fraudulently, with an identity she'd been forced to manufacture for herself—okay, okay, the identity she'd been forced to steal for herself—Emma didn't doubt that she would indeed enjoy living here at the bed-and-breakfast. The bus from Ithaca hadn't come as far as Sudbury—she'd had to walk the final mile—and its isolation alone was enough to make her fall in love with the place. Then she'd entered the town proper and found a place almost trapped in time, full of quaint shops and charming houses and a few honest-to-God cobbled streets. She'd had just enough money left in her pocket to buy lunch at a place that looked like something straight out of an old movie, where a waitress named Marge, who could have been her grandmother—had she ever actually had a grandmother, she meant—called her "doll." Afterward she'd stumbled upon a street vendor selling frozen treats and bought an old-fashioned Dreamsicle for dessert.

If she hadn't seen the village for herself, had someone described it to her, Emma never would have believed it was real. Sudbury, New York, wasn't like anyplace she'd ever lived before or like anyplace she would have ever expressed a desire to live. No one was going to find her here. No one.

Just as long as she remained vigilant. And as long as she stayed offline.

Pax Lightfoot was early for his meeting with Haven Moreau at Summerlight, but that was nothing new, so she was probably expecting him. Especially since he'd told her during their call the day before that he had some excellent news about the inn's launch this fall. Launching Summerlight on social media was, after all, the reason Haven had hired him. And as side hustles went, he was more than a little fond of this one. Sure, teaching computer and information science at Cornell was his bread and butter, not to mention the wave of the future. But Pax had a soft spot for old stuff, too.

Old music. Old movies. Old clothes. Old houses. And Summerlight…

As he always did when he arrived on-site, he took a minute to appreciate the gorgeous French Renaissance Revival mansion. All four floors of it. He should have probably been appalled by the fact that places like this had only been possible thanks to a time of incredible wealth and social disparity. And yeah, okay, most of him was appalled by that. But another part of him remained in awe that such exuberant beauty had come about in a world like that to begin with. And that it still stood as a testament to that time a century after its creators were gone. Too many of these carpetbagger mansions had been chopped up into little pieces or flat out torn down in the name of progress.

Summerlight might have succumbed to the same fate had its current owners not stepped in when they did. The first time Pax visited, the place had looked like it was on its last legs. Desolate and battered against a bleak winter sky, it had barely looked fit for habitation. Even the insides of the house had been neglected and ragged at that point. Now, though, the mansion had been reborn, sparkling in the summer sunlight like a jewel in the tiara of a nineteenth-century debutante. Haven and Bennett really had brought the house back to life since inheriting it.

And Pax couldn't help feeling like he was a part of its revival. Because after Haven hired him to be Summerlight's social media guy just before Christmas, he'd been the one to get the word out online that had brought in a boatload of cash and turned things around for the house that would be her and Bennett's home as well as their livelihood. Thanks to Pax, it was booked solid for the first six months after its opening. At the rate he was creating buzz for the place, the inn would never have a vacant room again. If he had his way, it was going to be in business for another century at least.

Of course, once the fall semester started at Cornell in a couple of months and he had to go back to teaching, he would have to juggle two jobs again. But for now, with summer just unfolding, he could give the bulk of his attention to whatever Haven and Bennett needed doing. That the *doing* part just so happened to include frequent visits to a gorgeous Gilded Age mansion was his favorite perk of the job.

He made his way up the steps to the front door and, as he always did when visiting, opened it and strode right in. Haven had told him to make himself at home here the day she hired him. She'd even given him unfettered use of the desktop in her office to use for a workspace whenever he was here. And, thankfully, she was even more casual than he was when it came to office attire, so him being dressed in his standard uniform of khaki cargo pants and a vintage camp shirt—this one spattered with mai tais and cockatoos—would be no problem. She was probably in the office right now waiting for him, despite his earlier-than-planned arrival. He turned to make his way down the east-wing hallway, past the library, reading room, and breakfast room, to take the last turn on the left into the office, and—

And stop dead in his tracks. Because it wasn't Haven waiting for him in there. It was…someone else. Someone bathed in a splash of golden sunlight that gave her an otherworldly glow. Had Pax been a religious man, he would have called the creature before him heavenly. Truly. With her soft brown hair and creamy skin, dressed in a flowing floral skirt and oversize T-shirt, there was just something kind of ethereal about her. Something kind of transcendent. Something kind of angelic. She was on a stepladder, shelving a book among scores of others in the built-in floor-to-ceiling shelves on the opposite side of the room, a position that gave her the appearance of floating in midair. Adding to his whimsical impression, the sunlight streaming through a nearby window pooled on the crown of her head, giving the impression of a halo.

If angels really did exist, this woman would be a member of the highest order, such was her embodiment of Truth and Beauty. And that was saying something, since truth was, to Pax, the most sacred thing in the world. Having been raised by a family of con artists— ones who made their living by lying to and using people, and who enlisted their children in their scams the minute they were old enough to be useful—truth was the one thing on which he never, *ever* compromised. On which he *would* never, *ever* compromise. Truth was everything to Pax. There was never a good reason for lying. People who lied either did so to manipulate others or to hide something awful about themselves. He knew that from experience, had seen it over and over again when he was growing up. Dishonesty was a blight on humanity. He would have no part of it in his life these days.

As if he'd just spoken his credo aloud, the angel on

the ladder turned suddenly to look at him…and made every thought he might have entertained for the next few minutes…or hours…or centuries…evaporate. Full-on, she was even more beautiful and brilliant than she was in profile. Long bangs fell to just above her eyes, making her seem a bit more mischievous than an angel would be. *Maybe she's a fairy*, he thought. *Or a sprite.* Whoever, whatever she was, she was definitely something from another, better, world than this one.

It was all he could do to say "Hello."

She only gazed at him in silence for a moment. Then, very softly, very quickly, she replied, "Hi."

But the tiny word came out sounding uncertain and whispery, as if this was her first time speaking aloud. And her expression, he couldn't help thinking, was a little panicked, as if she were indeed a fey being he'd just caught in the act of fairy mischief, and she was about to disappear, like that, in a puff of smoke.

Oh, get a grip, he told himself. What the hell was wrong with him, thinking this way? He was a man of science and technology, not some raging poet seeing muses and magic everywhere. Whoever this woman was, as beautiful as she was, she was no angel. Or fairy or sprite, for that matter. Probably. Okay, maybe.

Anyway.

"I was looking for Haven," he told the angel. Uh, woman.

"She had to run into Sudbury," the angel-woman replied. "She said she'd be back by ten."

Which was when Pax was supposed to meet her. He glanced at his watch. Still fifteen minutes away.

He looked at the woman again, thinking she'd come down from the ladder and introduce herself. But she did neither. She only continued to stare at him with her overly large eyes—Were they really golden, or was that just the light playing tricks?—still looking as if she wanted to be anywhere but here. When he took a few more steps into the office, she looked even more alarmed. There had never been such a perfect example of *deer in the headlights*.

He stopped in the middle of the room and did his best to be nonthreatening. Not that he was ever threatening to begin with—he was the most easygoing person in the world—but something about this woman made him think she felt threatened by his simple existence. He ran a quick hand through his dark hair, rubbed his knuckles lightly over his beard and shoved his hands deep into his trouser pockets. Then he rocked back on his heels and said, "I'm Pax. Pax Lightfoot. I'm the inn's social media guy."

He had thought his introduction would put her at ease. Instead, she looked even more alarmed. She did step carefully off the ladder, though—never once unlocking her gaze from his—and take a few steps forward. But the moment she started to draw close to him, she sidestepped to position herself behind Haven's desk, as if she wanted—or even needed—to keep a physical barrier between them.

"I'm Emma," she told him. But she didn't give him a last name. "I just started working here this week. I'm the new housekeeper."

He remembered now how excited Haven had been

when she told him she'd hired the first of what would be a trio of full-time employees for Summerlight. What she hadn't told him was that she'd be hiring such a paragon of virtue.

Grip, Pax reminded himself. *Get one. Now.*

"It's nice to meet you, Emma," he said. "You're going to like it here. Haven and Bennett are great to work for. Do you live in Sudbury?"

She shook her head. "I live here at Summerlight. Upstairs. In what Haven told me are the old servants' quarters."

"Right. She said they were going to include room and board in the gig," he recalled. "So where are you from originally?"

She hesitated for a telling moment, then replied evasively, "Here and there."

Here and there. That was what Pax had always said about himself before settling in Ithaca as a student a decade ago. Of course, it hadn't been an ambiguous figure of speech for him the way he suspected it was for Emma. Although he'd been born in Louisiana—at least, that was what his parents had told him—he had no memory of the place because he hadn't lived there long. The birth certificate he had was from that state, but for all he knew, his parents had forged it—or even stolen it from someone—so who knew for sure? He'd never lived anywhere for long, though; that was for sure. By the time he left home at seventeen, he'd resided in every single one of the contiguous states at one point or another. In Canada and Mexico for a while, too. He wondered how many *here*s and *there*s Emma had called home. Maybe they could compare notes sometime.

"Where most recently?" he asked. He was just making conversation until Haven returned, and he had no idea what kinds of things angels usually talked about.

There was another one of those telling hesitations, then she seemed to relax. A little. She seemed to be forcing herself to do it, but at least she did seem to unclench a bit. She moved out from behind the desk and took a few more steps forward. But she stopped when a good five feet of floor still separated them. She also crossed her arms over her midsection, a clearly defensive gesture. Or maybe even one of self-preservation. Then she took a fortifying breath and smiled. Almost genuinely, too.

"Most recently, I'm from Scranton," she finally said.

Pax nodded. "I've been there. My family lived in the Hill, a few blocks north of Mulberry Street. What part of town did you call home?"

Her smile dropped, and she seemed to hold herself tighter. "Um, actually, not far from there at all. But I'm originally from Altoona," she quickly added. "Which is also in Pennsylvania."

Yeah, Pax kinda knew that.

She hurried on again: "It's the home of Hedda Hopper and the original horseshoe curve, birthplace of Georgism, and sister city to St. Pölten, Austria."

Okay, Pax didn't know that. That was very…informative. About Altoona anyway. What he really wanted to know more about was Emma-with-no-last-name who'd lived here and there. Before he could ask her anything that might enlighten him that way, though—other than the Scranton and Altoona stuff—she turned the tables on him.

"Where are you from?" she asked.

He gave his standard answer. "Lots of places." Emma wasn't the only one who could be ambiguous. *So there.*

She smiled again, and this time the gesture was more sincere, lighting her features as brightly as the sunlight had before she stepped out of it. Her eyes—more tawny than golden, he realized now that she was closer—fairly glowed with good humor, giving her whole person a luminosity Pax would have sworn couldn't exist outside an Edison bulb. He did his best not to swoon.

"Where most recently?" she asked, mimicking his own query.

"Ithaca," he told her. "It's where I live now."

"And where are you from originally?"

He blew out a restless breath. "Shreveport, Louisiana. At least that's what my birth certificate says and what my parents told me. But I'm not sure either one of them ever spoke an honest word in their life. There are times when I'm not even sure they were really my actual parents, and I haven't seen or spoken to them for fifteen years, so…"

Which was true. In the group of scammers he'd grown up with, everyone had seemed to be related to everyone else, sometimes in ways that were nebulous at best. Words like *aunt* and *uncle* and *ma* and *pa* had been thrown about with little distinction, and don't even get him started on words like *brother*, *sister*, and *cousin*. The way he'd grown up, families had been fluid and children had sometimes drifted from one couple to another and back again. Although Pax had borne a strong resemblance to his father—physically anyway—he didn't really have much solid proof of his actual lineage. And since lying had been the norm for everyone he'd grown up with, there was just no way to know for sure.

At his revelation, Emma's brows arrowed downward for a moment, almost as if she felt a kind of kinship for him. "You're estranged from your family?"

"If you want to put it politely like that, sure," Pax said. He actually felt more like he'd escaped his family. *Tomato, tomahto.*

"I'm not in contact with my parents, either," she told him. Then she looked surprised that she had revealed that. "I mean…" She blew out an exasperated sound. "It was nothing major. We were just never close." She quickly added, "So you live in Ithaca now," deftly changing the subject.

He nodded. "For about ten years. I got my MS and PhD at Cornell and have been teaching there for the past five years."

"What do you teach?"

"Computer and information science."

As quickly as the light had gone on inside Emma, it died completely. And where she'd seemed to be coming out of the protective shell she'd erected—she'd even dropped the arms she'd had crossed in front of herself— she immediately retreated, wrapping herself in those arms again, even tighter than before. He might as well have just told her he made his living as an axe murderer, so complete was her withdrawal. She took three giant steps to her right, then a half dozen even bigger steps forward, toward the door. Again, her eyes never left his. But her stride hastened with every movement she made.

"I see," she said. "Well. So. Then. Um. I just remembered something I need to be doing. Somewhere else," she continued, the words coming even more hastily and jerkily than her movements. "In another part of the house. I'm sure Haven will be back any minute. It was great meeting you. Have a nice day."

There might as well have been a puff of smoke to accompany her exit—that was how abruptly and completely she disappeared. All Pax could do was stand in place, looking at the spot from which she'd vanished, his head full again with thoughts of truth and beauty... and magic and mayhem.

And staring at the door, wondering just who the hell Emma-with-no-last-name from here-and-there really was.

Chapter Two

Emma somehow managed to make it to the kitchen before her legs buckled beneath her. She clung to a countertop long enough to steady herself, then threw open a cabinet door to frantically snatch a tumbler from inside. After filling it with water from the tap, she gulped down half, then reminded herself to breathe. In, out. In, out. In…out…in…out. She closed her eyes, inhaled and exhaled a few more deep breaths, then opened them again. Outside the window over the sink, the lake she'd already come to love glittered in the late-morning sunlight. The sky was bright blue and streaked with wisps of clouds, and a soft breeze ruffled the leaves of the trees at the edge of the yard. A small gray bird settled on the windowsill long enough to chirp at her, then flew away again. It was as peaceful a scene as any imaginary one she could have conjured in her mind, something she'd done over the past nine months every time she'd felt panic about to overtake her. But instead of absorbing the genuine serenity beyond the window, her brain was clattering with the cacophony of a thousand frenetic thoughts.

It made sense that the inn where she would be working for the foreseeable future would have a social media guy. It made even more sense that said media guy would be an expert in all things computer-and-information related, enough so that he was able to teach at a tony Ivy League school. It made sense that her path would cross with his at some point. But wow, none of those sensible things had crossed her mind when she'd accepted the job at Summerlight. It just went to show how very far from her element she had strayed since last fall.

She really should have seen a problem like Pax Lightfoot coming. She should have realized Sudbury, New York, was too good to be true. She should have known better than to think she could take up actual residence somewhere and remain undetected. She just wished it could have taken more than a few days for everything to come crashing down around her again. It had taken less than a week for her to fall in love with this place. Her little room upstairs felt more like home to her than any of her actual places of residence ever had. Not that that was really saying much, since *happy home life* was a phrase that had never been a part of her lexicon, but still. Within hours of unpacking the other day, Emma had honestly started to feel as if she could spend the rest of her life here—and happily, at that.

She downed another few swallows of water, took a few more fortifying breaths and reminded herself that Pax Lightfoot, social media guy/computer-and-information-science professor, hadn't recognized her. At all. And he was exactly the type who *should* have recognized her. He should have taken one look at her, mumbled some excuse for why he had to suddenly leave, then gone out into the hall to make a phone call. If he had recognized her, it would have been worth six figures for him to turn her in. Six figures and hero status in every testosterone-driven, woman-hating forum in the manosphere, a collection of anti-feminist, misogynistic entities on the internet. In other words, the bane of her existence. If he had recognized her, he would have been a tech bro among tech bros and king of the neckbeards. If he had recognized her, his name would have been chiseled into the digital landscape of the hypermasculine—at least to their way of thinking—for millennia.

If he had recognized her.

But he hadn't. Even when she had gotten closer to him than almost anyone she'd encountered for months, he hadn't recognized her. Even when she had spoken to him, he hadn't recognized her. And she'd gotten closer and spoken to him *voluntarily*, she marveled. She'd even spoken at length to him. She'd told him something personal about her childhood home life, for God's sake. What was up with that?

Oh, right. Loneliness. That could make a person do and say things they didn't mean to do or say. Especially after months and months and months of it. She truly hadn't realized how lonely she'd become until this week. Speaking in brief spurts with Haven on a completely professional level had made her feel as if she'd reunited with long-lost family. Which was a laugh, since Emma's family had just been three people keeping their distance from each other under the same roof. She didn't even know what family was. But having lived so long with no one in her life, sharing space and conversation with her employer this week had felt like the most intimate sharing she could have with someone.

Loneliness sucked. But it was no excuse, Emma told herself, for letting down her guard, even for just a few minutes. Lots of people were lonely. But they still had the presence of mind to keep themselves safe. Pax Lightfoot was the last sort of person she should be getting close to—physically or socially. Because if he recognized her…

But he hadn't, she reminded herself again. Not right off the bat anyway. Of course, Emma had made damned sure by now that no one *would* recognize her, but she still hadn't been confident her efforts were successful. This time last year, she'd had electric-blue hair and a killer hand with lipsticks and highlighters, with contour brushes and exotic eyeliners. So killer that her cosmetics forum on TikTok had numbered nearly eighty thousand followers—and that number had been growing by leaps and bounds. Her wardrobe had consisted exclusively of black and neons, the bulk of it corsets, fishnets and Doc Martens. She'd never left the house without at least a dozen bracelets and a half dozen earrings, most of them the size of Rhode Island.

And, of course, this time last year, her name hadn't been Emma Brown. It had been Amber Finch. A name that really would be chiseled into the digital landscape for millennia. Except in Amber's case, it wasn't for an act of misguided—and misogynistic—heroism, the way it would have been for any guy who found her and turned her in. In her case, it was for being an articulate, gutsy woman—okay, some might have said loudmouthed and obnoxious, and, okay, they wouldn't necessarily have been wrong—who made a toxic-masculinity guru with millions of followers look like a raging idiot.

In the online world, Travis Swope was a god among men—men who couldn't get a date to save their lives. Ironically because they lived their lives according to Travis Swope's "advice," the bulk of which was about how to treat women—specifically as sexual house-keeping objects to be subjugated by men. His acolytes were… Hmm. How did one describe a bunch of stupid, hateful, nasty pieces of work politely? Then again, why be polite to a bunch of stupid, hateful, nasty pieces of work? Swope's cult of flying monkeys ranged from woman-haters at best to sex offenders at worst. And every last one of them wanted Amber Finch's head—and other choice body parts—on a silver platter to turn over to their king. All because she kicked out from beneath him—with a vengeance—the pedestal on which they'd placed their idol, Travis Swope.

In hindsight, it maybe hadn't been such a good idea for Amber Finch, marginally successful online makeup artist and super successful tech-security pro, to take on Travis Swope, king of the incels, especially on his own social media. But she hadn't been able to help herself when a particularly odious bit of his woman-hating philosophy went viral. Naturally, she'd gone in under her anonymous online handle, Litha Firefly, since Swope's followers were notoriously vicious. Not only had Amber, as Litha, taken Travis on, she had taken him *down*. Brutally. The exchange between the two of

them in the comments of his vlog had lasted maybe
ten minutes, tops. But it had been a ferocious annihi-
lation on Amber's part, and before the day was out, it
had gone even more viral than his hateful advice had.

What had also quickly gone viral was Travis Swope's
out-and-out fury at being so thoroughly bested by a
woman—not that he for a moment admitted that he
had been bested by a woman. Litha Firefly was just
some crazy bitch who'd overstepped and needed to be
put in her place—that was all. The sooner, the better.

To do that, Travis put a six-figure bounty on Litha
Firefly's head. One hundred thousand dollars to anyone
who could identify the uppity woman who had "tried"
to make him look bad and bring her to him at his Las
Vegas party mansion. Presumably alive—though, honestly, that part had never really been specified. Fortu-
nately Amber had made her living in tech security and
was a first-rate cyber hacker herself. She'd ensured that
Litha Firefly would always *stay* anonymous when she
was online.

It hadn't been long, though, before someone who was
also good with tech made the connection between Litha
Firefly and Amber Finch. And that someone plastered
photos all over the web of both her and a unique, very
large tattoo she had on her back, all lifted from her social media. Once Litha was outed as Amber online for
all the world—and for all of Travis Swope's minions—
to see… Well. Things had gotten ugly fast. To put it
mildly. The flood began with hateful comments on her
makeup vlog and personal accounts, calling her every
derogatory name a woman could be called—and wow,

there were *a lot* of derogatory words for women, she'd
been alarmed to realize. Then came the emails and IMs
full of death and rape threats. Those were quickly followed by deepfake porno videos featuring her and a
variety of partners, often at the same time.

As scary as all of that had been, though, Amber had
still been confident she was tech-savvy enough to keep
herself safe. But to paraphrase Qui-Gon Jinn, there was
always a bigger fish. Someone more tech-savvy than she
was found her address and phone number and plastered
those all over the web, too, for Travis Swope's army of
scumbags to see.

And oh, how those scumbags had come for her, with
phone calls and texts that seemed even more vicious
than the online threats, because they hit so much closer
to home. Literally. Nearly every time Amber tried to
leave her high-security building, one—or more—of
Swope's followers would be out on the doorstep waiting for her.

Nausea rolled through Emma's stomach now as she
replayed those early days in her head. It had helped
enormously that every photo of her on the web was one
where she was in full makeup, from false eyelashes to
contoured cheeks to plumped-up lips. So simply washing her face before heading out anywhere had gone a
long way toward hiding her identity. Still, her blue hair
and especially her tattoo—a symbol of the Triple Goddess entwined with a tree of life that spanned her back
from one shoulder blade to the other—would peg her as
public enemy number one with Swope's scumbag army.

So she'd always made sure to wear a hat and shirt with sleeves, as well, if she went out.

She'd been confident, too, that she would be able to protect her identity beyond her front door until the insanity of the bounty on her head calmed down and the manosphere turned its hatred to one of the shiny new outrages du jour that seemed to crop up with them daily. The manosphere really did seem to like outrages du jour, after all. Alas, she had sorely overestimated her confidence—or, more likely, had sorely underestimated the manosphere. Because Travis Swope made it his life's work to find and destroy Amber Finch. He posted daily "Amber alerts" and offered prizes to anyone who could make her life hell in whatever way possible.

It started with her none-too-shabby bank account being hacked and drained and culminated with a gaggle of Swope's followers somehow getting into her building and pounding on her front door. Then they started throwing their weight against it. Amber had just enough time to grab her phone and wallet before the door began to splinter. Then she bolted through the back door in her kitchen, into a different hallway, and raced down five flights of steps to the street below.

She spent that first night with a friend and waited a full day before returning to her condo, only to find it inhabited by the very goons who had forced their way in. She called the cops, who came and removed them, then she had her door repaired and reinforced and new locks added to the old. It did no good. Because there were plenty of other goons out there doing Travis Swope's bidding, and soon more came to her front door. Then more after them. Then more after them. The cops finally washed their hands of Amber and her complaints, telling her it was a civil matter that she'd need to take up on her own. Which was total BS, but what could she do when no one replied to her many, many, *many* calls of people trying to break into her home? The bank, too, told her there was nothing they could do about her lost funds—*so sad, too bad.* She was left without recourse, wondering just how the hell she was supposed to get herself out of the jam she'd created for herself when no one would even try to help her.

It quickly became clear that she would not be getting herself out of the jam she'd created for herself. Because her persecutors got the word out that Amber Finch had changed her looks and posted fuzzy photos of her in hats and sunglasses exiting her building. Not only had she been continuously recognized in Seattle, she'd also been followed and jeered at and chased. And, in one terrifying case, physically attacked by three men twice her size. It was only thanks to a couple of passersby that she escaped what could have been an unspeakable assault by a trio of Swope's fanboys.

After that, Amber knew she was going to have to disappear from both private and public life until the Travis Swope hysteria calmed down. But it didn't calm down. Swope's demand for her only grew, along with the bounty for her, which eventually doubled. For a few weeks, she was able to couch surf with her handful of friends, since she dared not return to her condo and had no funds for a hotel. But every time she went out in public, someone spotted her. And harassed her. And followed her back to wherever she was staying.

Ultimately, she realized she couldn't risk endangering her friends as she had endangered herself. So she told them all she was leaving Seattle and would be in touch when she could. They were kind enough to pool what cash they could to get her started, much of which she used to buy a burner phone and her first bus ticket out of town. But even as she made her way to Butte, she was recognized by another traveler and heckled the whole way. She knew then that she would never be safe anywhere as long as she was Amber Finch.

So once in Butte, she dyed her hair back to its original soft brown and gave herself some bangs, and she stopped wearing makeup entirely. She ditched her punk-rock-girl outfits and thrifted a few pieces more suited to an earth-mother goddess. There was nothing she could do about the tattoo on her back—her brand now, such as it was—except hide it. So she for damned sure made certain not a speck of it was ever showing.

None of that helped, though, as long as she bore the name Amber Finch. But because she was so good at manipulating tech, she was able to steal the identity of someone else—Emma Brown, of Altoona, Pennsylvania. A young woman who was close to Amber in age but had almost no online presence and a wonderfully common name. The Emma Brown she chose to imitate, Amber had figured, would never know if someone else was out there posing as her. People generally never knew when their identity was stolen until it was used for theft, and Amber had no intention of stealing anything more from Emma than her name and history.

Even more to the point, Amber, as Emma, didn't intend to have an online presence, either. By now, she had hacked enough websites—both public and private—to make her version of Emma Brown look like a reality. And look like Amber, too. She was no slouch at Photoshop, so she'd been able to substitute her own face with Emma's in the few places Emma had appeared online. Anyone looking into Emma Brown's background—because at some point, Amber/Emma was going to have to find a job, since who knew how long she would have to be in hiding—would see that she at least *looked* legit. So far, so good.

Thankfully, nine months after Amber's initial outing, things had settled down to some degree. Most of the online mob searching for Litha Firefly/Amber Finch had grown bored by now and had found other women to bully from the privacy of their moms' basements. But there was still enough chatter about her on the web, and she'd still had enough close calls over the past few months, to make her more than a little twitchy. Six figures would go a long way for a lot of people. So would digital fame. And there were a lot of creeps who would simply do anything to endear themselves to Travis Swope. Emma was in no way ready to let her guard down, nor would she be anytime soon. Some of those guys were flat-out nuts.

Until she could be absolutely certain of her safety, she would do and say whatever she had to in order to stay Emma Brown of Altoona, Pennsylvania. She just hoped that didn't wind up being the name on her gravestone.

Pax Lightfoot, however, didn't seem to be one of the guys looking for her, she thought now. At least meeting him hadn't been one of those close calls. Considering what he did for a living, he must spend a lot of time on the internet. There was no way he didn't know who Amber Finch was, and he had to be aware what she looked like, right down to the Triple Goddess–tree of life tattoo that spanned her upper back. Photos of her and that image showed up in new forums almost daily. She knew that from the weekly forays she made online—from public computers—to see how bad the heat on her still was. The bounty on her head had reached far beyond the dregs-dwelling parts of the internet where Travis Swope's minions lived. It had made headlines in some places last fall, and it still cropped up in online conversations.

Pax had to know all about what had happened to Litha/Amber, and he must be hearing the buzz that continued to haunt every corner of social media even now. But he had greeted Emma Brown in as warm and friendly a manner as could be.

He hadn't recognized her. Yet. Although the photos of her online bore almost no resemblance to the woman she was now, that hadn't stopped a few eagle-eyed guys from recognizing her anyway, as recently as last month. Pax Lightfoot might very well turn out to be another one who did, especially if she spent any length of time with him. So she was going to have to make sure she spent as little time with him as possible.

Too bad, too. He was super cute. Now that she had stopped panicking, she could admit that. *Tall, dark and handsome* was far too clichéd to describe his appeal. His dark hair was rakishly in need of a cut, and his eyes had been the color of bittersweet chocolate behind his geek-chic glasses. Her favorite color combination on a guy. He was nearly a foot taller than she, his shoulders and biceps straining enough against his shirt to make clear that everything else lurking underneath was solid muscle. His beard was tidy enough that she could tell he took care of it, but scruffy enough that he didn't seem to be overly fastidious. And the retro camp shirt, likewise just rumpled enough to assure her he wasn't all that concerned with his image, had made him that much sexier to her.

Oh, yeah. She could have—would have—totally gone for him in her previous life. Gorgeous. Solid. Funny. Smart. He was exactly her type.

No, he isn't, she immediately corrected herself. Pax Lightfoot was Amber Finch's type. He wasn't Emma Brown's type. Emma's type was... Invisible. Nonexistent. Emma couldn't afford to have a type. Every guy she met could be a potential Travis Swope bootlicker. There were millions of them out there. Her path had already crossed with enough of them to convince her they could and would do her harm. No way was she going to risk throwing herself in the path of one of them again.

Emma would keep her distance from Pax Lightfoot. She simply couldn't afford not to. And if she *did* run into him again here at Summerlight, she would just ensure that Emma Brown was the antithesis of Amber

Finch so he'd never suspect otherwise. Amber had been brash, mouthy and impulsive. She hadn't cared who she offended or how the world saw her. Well, not until the world saw her all over the place and turned on her. So Emma would be the opposite of Amber—reserved, quiet and careful of every word that came out of her mouth.

She inhaled another deep breath and released it slowly. She had to keep reminding herself that, for now, she was safe. There was little chance she would see much of Pax here at Summerlight anyway. She probably wouldn't run into him at all after today, since he would have no reason to interact with the inn's housekeeper. And God knew she wasn't going to be traveling beyond Sudbury while she was here. Still, it might not be a bad idea for her to put an escape plan into place. Again. Be ready to leave at a moment's notice and go...somewhere.

Emma would figure it out. She always did. It wasn't just the past nine months that had thrown obstacles in her path. Her life had been full of them. She would just do what she had always done—take one step forward at a time while constantly watching her back. She'd survive. She always did.

She just wished that, for once, she could breathe easy for more than a few days.

"So that's where we are," Pax told Haven as he wound up their meeting a half hour after starting it. "Everything is on track for the holiday opening of Summerlight the weekend before Thanksgiving. I think you're going to be really pleased with how it all goes."

"Thanks to you," Haven told him. "I don't know where Bennett and I would be if it weren't for you."

Pax was grateful for the kudos, and yeah, okay, he'd done a lot. But he was being paid well for his work. And it wasn't like Haven hadn't done anything. Her love for this house was really what had brought it back to life.

"Thanks," he told her. "But you and Bennett are the real driving forces for this place. I had no idea Summerlight was even here, so close to me, until you two started working on it. So many of these Gilded Age mansions have been torn down due to neglect or to subdivide the properties. I'm glad this one isn't going to suffer the same fate."

"No way could I let that happen," Haven said with a smile. "From the minute I entered it, I knew this house was special. I'm just glad I finally got Bennett on board to rehab it instead of tear it down for a shiny new resort. It really has been a labor of love."

Pax and Haven made chitchat as he closed his laptop and tucked it back into his battered leather messenger bag. How Haven was thinking about expanding the garden and looking into organizing lake excursions and nature hikes. How Pax had an idea for a new page on the website that focused on the inn's rehabilitation, if Haven didn't mind sharing some of her own photographic journey for that.

Then, out of nowhere, he heard himself ask, "So. Emma. How's she working out?"

Haven looked as surprised at hearing the question as Pax had been asking it. He had no idea what had caused that to pop out of his mouth. Then she smiled.

"You met our new housekeeper, did you?"

He nodded. "She was in the office working when I came in. She seems very nice."

Haven nodded, her smile growing broader. "Nice," she echoed. "Right. Cute, too, huh?"

"That's not what I meant at all," Pax assured her.

"Oh, really."

Her response was a statement, not a question. So Pax didn't respond to it. "I just thought you were going to wait a bit longer before you started hiring your staff, that's all."

Her expression indicated she didn't believe for a moment that his interest was passive. Even so, she replied, "I was originally. But then I figured we were far along enough in the renovations that we should probably go ahead and have someone to take care of the parts of the house that are finished. I mean, it *is* a big house to keep clean, even with no one staying here yet. I didn't want our progress to get neglected before we even open. And there are still a few jobs to do around here that are too small a task for professionals to be interested in but a layperson can do just fine. Emma will be great for those."

That surprised Pax. "Does she have experience renovating houses?"

"Not really," Haven said. "Her résumé was pretty eclectic."

"In what way?"

Haven smiled again. "She must have really made an impression on you."

He wanted to object but knew that would be lying.

So he only said, "Idle curiosity." Which was true. Well, maybe he was more actively curious than idly, but still. "We just had a nice chat. She didn't even tell me her last name."

He waited to see if Haven would fill in that blank for him. But she only continued to smile in a way that told him she wasn't buying his detachment at all. Okay, so sue him—Emma was pretty cute.

"She was a waitress at a diner in Scranton before she came here," Haven told him. "She's actually been a waitress a lot. And a bartender. And a salesclerk and a cashier. And an editorial assistant. But she worked as a housekeeper at a boutique hotel in Carlisle, Pennsylvania, while she was working on her BA at Dickinson College, so that was good enough for me."

Pax found it odd that Emma had attended Dickinson but was only working as a housekeeper at this point and had held a host of other menial jobs. Not that working in a menial job was anything to be ashamed of—hell, he'd worked plenty of them himself—but Dickinson wasn't exactly an inexpensive school, and it had an excellent reputation. A degree from there could open a lot of doors.

"What was her major at Dickinson?" he asked.

"English," Haven said.

Oh, well. That explained it.

She added, "But she's enthusiastic and happy to take on whatever project I throw at her. She even likes her tiny room upstairs. She's gonna be great here."

Pax didn't doubt that for a minute. He just wished he could come up with some excuses for why he could be here at Summerlight more often himself. Unfortunately, after today, there was nothing to bring him back to the inn for a while. Well, nothing but Emma. Whose last name he still didn't know, since Haven wasn't being any help there, even if she knew him well enough by now to know that he wasn't a creep. He guessed women couldn't be too careful these days. Most of them probably looked out for each other regardless.

He and Haven said their farewells, then he headed back down the hall toward the front door. He told himself he was *not* looking for Emma as he glanced into every room he passed on his way out. He wasn't. He was just marveling at how far along the house had come since the first time he entered it. Haven had done her best to preserve as many period details as she could, and she'd done an amazing job recreating them where preservation had been impossible. The walls of every room bore the rich blues and greens of that time or even richer wallpaper. Virtually all the furnishings were original to the house because it had stayed in either Haven's or Bennett's families since its construction. The battered wood floors had been refinished, the cracked marble had been repaired, the broken tiles had been replaced. And—

And oh, hey, whaddaya know, there was Emma, in the massive foyer. She was on a ladder again, this one ten times as tall as the one in Haven's office. And she was at the very top of it, wiping clean what looked like thousands of prisms on the colossal chandelier hanging over it all. Seriously, she must have been twenty feet up. Not wearing a safety harness or anything. What the hell was she thinking? Yeah, her feet were planted firmly on the third rung down, and her thighs were pressed securely against the ladder's top. But she might as well have been washing windows on the Chrysler Building, so precarious was the situation overall.

"You know, you really shouldn't be up on a ladder that high when you're all alone," he said before he could stop himself, his voice echoing ominously back in the otherwise empty space. What was it about her that made his mouth work faster than his brain?

She flinched when he spoke, and he thought for a second that she was going to tumble backward. He rushed to the foot of the ladder to catch her, but she caught herself effortlessly instead and righted herself with no problem.

"I was fine until some idiot started yammering at me," she growled down at him.

Okay, he'd had that coming. Even so, she seemed to recognize her bad temper, because her expression immediately softened.

"I'm sorry," she said. Though she seemed to be talking to the room at large, not him specifically. She'd moved her gaze from him to the sweeping staircase to his left. "I didn't mean to snap. You're not an idiot. I apologize."

Though somehow he got the impression that she did, in fact, consider him an idiot but was worried more about how he might take the aspersion.

"No, *I* apologize," he told her. "I shouldn't have startled you."

She looked down at him again, long enough for him

to think she expected him to say something else. When Pax offered no indication that he had any idea what that expectation might have been—mostly because he had no idea what she might have been expecting—she looked meaningfully at the front door, then more meaningfully back at him. Then the door again. Then him. Right. She was waiting for him to leave. But how could he leave when she was way up on top of a ladder where she shouldn't be without a spotter?

"I'll wait until you're done," he told her. "It really isn't a good idea to be that far up there all alone. I mean, one misstep, and you're toast. Or, rather, a big pile of marmalade that would be good on toast. If it weren't for the fact that it was made out of splattered human being, I mean."

He wasn't sure, but he thought she bit back a smile at that. Hard to tell with her halfway to Heaven like she was.

"I'll be fine," she assured him, her tone a little softer than before but still edged with something barely restrained. "I've been fine on this ladder all week. This isn't the only ginormous chandelier in this house, and this won't be the last time I'm cleaning one. It's okay. I promise."

"Maybe," he said. "But until there are more people *in* this house to help if you fall…"

"I'll be fine," she repeated.

Oh, she was already fine, Pax thought. More than fine. She was an angel of Truth and Beauty. And he intended to make sure she stayed one of those and not an actual angel that came about because she took a tumble from a ladder as tall as the Chrysler Building.

"I'm not going anywhere until you're done," he assured her.

She expelled a sound of derision. "Fine. I'm done."

To prove that, she began stepping down, rung by careful rung. Unable to help himself, Pax held the ladder in place until she was safely back on the ground. Of course, that meant that once she was on the ground, she was standing mere inches away from him. But his original intentions had had nothing to do with that. Honest.

The minute she realized she was, in fact, mere inches away from him, Emma took a few steps backward until there were a few feet—and also the ladder—separating them. But that was okay. From where he stood, Pax could still see the warmth in her eyes and the ghost of a reluctant smile that played around her mouth. She wasn't quite as relaxed or happy as she appeared, however. There was something anxious and wary buzzing around her, as if she were poised to vanish in a puff of smoke again, the way she had been in the office earlier. Why was she so skittish?

"There," she told him. "I'm okay. You can leave now." As if she realized how rude she was being again, she added, "I mean, I know you were on your way out. I don't want to hold you up any longer than I already have. You must have a million other places to be. No need to be wasting time with little ol' me."

There was something odd about her delivery, Pax couldn't help thinking. Like she was trying to be demure and accommodating but actually had no idea how to be either.

As if to punctuate that dichotomy, she added, "Off you go, then. If you want to, I mean."

Pax didn't want to go. He had wanted to a few minutes ago, because he really did need to get back to Ithaca. Classes might not be starting again for another couple of months, but he had other side hustles besides Summerlight, not to mention a piece he was writing for *Wired* that was due in a week. But now that he was seeing these weird contradictions in her personality, he was even more intrigued than he'd been before.

"I actually don't have a million places to be," he told her. Which was true. Pax never lied. He really didn't have anywhere near a million places to be. Just two or three. "It's almost lunchtime. I was going to grab a sandwich in Sudbury before I head back to Ithaca." Also true. He loved the Italian sub at Jack's. He'd just been planning to take it to go—until now. His heartrate doubled as he asked, hopefully casually, "Any chance you'd like to come along?"

Her eyes widened in what he could only think went way beyond skittish. She looked full-out panicked now. Even more than she had in Haven's office a little while ago.

"No," she immediately, adamantly replied. Then, as she had before, she seemed to be trying to rein herself in, with not particularly good results. "I mean, thank you for the invitation. That's very kind of you. But I still have a lot to do before I can break for lunch."

Pax did his best not to be devastated by her turn-down. "Maybe another time, then," he said.

She nodded uneasily. "Mm-hmm," she squeaked as if she were being strangled. "Maybe."

He wouldn't go so far as to say her *Maybe* was a lie, even if it did seem like she was saying one thing when she meant another—that meaning being that she had no intention of even considering lunch with Pax at any point in the future. But she also wasn't ruling out the possibility of something like World War III happening at one of those points, and that might make them un-willing allies who were forced to share what limited rations they could dig up from a deserted gas station or something.

Hey, it could happen. Maybe. So she wasn't lying. Because if she was lying, she would no longer be an angel of Truth and Beauty.

Even more to the point, if she was lying, Pax could have nothing more to do with her. He really couldn't abide liars. He demanded honesty in every aspect of his life and with every person he encountered, the same way he was honest himself at all times. At the first whiff of deceit, he cut ties with a dishonest person, be their relationship personal or professional. Maybe that made him a jerk. Maybe it was unrealistic to expect anyone to be one hundred percent honest one hundred percent of the time. But everyone had their line in the sand. For Pax, it was truthfulness. If others couldn't toe that line, he wanted nothing to do with them.

So, in a way, Emma telling him that she might be open to lunch in the future when she obviously wasn't at the moment was her being authentic. Of course, it could also mean she had no interest in getting to know him better. But that was okay, too, he told himself. It was. Really. Sometimes people just didn't jibe for whatever reason. It was fine. He'd just met her, after all, and, as he'd been thinking earlier, there were few reasons why he'd even run into her again anytime soon. Pax would get over Emma not wanting to go out with him. Eventually.

He would. Really.

"Okay," he told her. "Then I'll leave you to your work." He made himself take a few steps toward the door but turned one last time to say, "It was nice meeting you, Emma."

She nodded. He thought she was going to say something along the lines of *You, too*, but she only smiled and lifted a hand in farewell. Probably, she didn't say something along the lines of *You, too* because she didn't want to be dishonest, since she hadn't exactly hidden the fact that Pax made her uncomfortable. What was weird, though, was that he also kind of got a vibe from her that, in other circumstances, she might have definitely taken him up on his offer of lunch.

Telling himself that that last thing was just wishful thinking, he, too, lifted a hand, then turned and made his way to the front door. This time he didn't look back, as much as he wanted to. There was no more room in his life for wishful thinking than there was for dishonesty. Because wishful thinking was about as productive as dishonesty was. Hell, wishful thinking was its own form of dishonesty. So yeah. No more of that for

Pax. No more wishful thinking about Emma-with-no-last-name.

In fact, no more thinking about Emma at all.

Chapter Three

At the end of Emma's second week of employment, she received something she hadn't received for a very long time—a regular paycheck. Although when she was living in Seattle, her side hustle as an online cosmetic maven had earned her a bit of money here and there, thanks to a handful of sponsors and advertisers, it hadn't been her chief source of income by any means. Her main job then had been as a self-employed computer-security tech, designing firewalls and programs to keep business's sites and social media safe from hackers like her. For that she had received payment for her services only sporadically, though those payments had generally been substantial. She hadn't received an actual paycheck since her years before settling in Seattle.

Even so, Emma was more proud of this paycheck than she'd been of any other remuneration. It was a symbol of how far she had come since last fall. After going on the run, she'd only taken jobs with the understanding that she would be paid in cash, under the table. Which, of course, meant her jobs had paid next to nothing and been shady at best. She'd mostly worked alongside others who were undocumented or also trying not to be found, usually in mom-and-pop-type establishments that had either been just starting up or on their last legs. Occasionally she'd accepted some assignment that was a one-time-only event—cleaning houses or garages or delivering things she didn't want to know the details about. But this...

This was an actual paycheck for an actual job. A job that, okay, she'd landed with a stolen identity. A stolen identity she'd also had to use to cash said check at Sudbury Community Bank with the phony Pennsylvania driver's license she'd bought from a friend in Seattle who made his living in questionable ways and who had wanted to help her out because *There but for the grace of God go I, Amber. There but for the grace of God, I tell you.* A stolen identity with which—or without which—she would have to break some federal laws when it came to filing taxes. Or, you know, not filing taxes. She'd worry about that in the spring.

Anyway, none of those things made her first paycheck from Summerlight any less valuable. So to mark the occasion, after cashing her first check, she decided to buy herself a celebratory lunch.

There had been a time in Emma's life when she wouldn't have given a second thought to going out for lunch. She'd done it a lot when she was Amber Finch. She might not have had a ton of friends in Seattle, but she'd had a handful, and she'd liked going out with them—and even spending extravagantly to do so. Her life growing up hadn't been the happiest. She'd been a late-life surprise to parents who'd never planned—or wanted—to have children. Her mother and father both had been born into poverty and stayed there. The arrival of a child had only strapped what little money they had even more. There had been no going out to lunch when Emma was growing up. There hadn't been any going anywhere at all. No summer vacations to fun tourist destinations. No themed—or any other kind of—birthday parties. No after-school activities or extra-curriculars. No visits from Santa or the Easter Bunny or the Tooth Fairy. There had only been struggling to get through the day with two people who wished she had never been born.

Emma had worked part-time jobs as a teenager to sock away what money she could, but she'd hidden that income from her parents, because she'd known they would demand she turn it over to them to pay them back for everything they'd spent on her. When she left home at eighteen after graduating from high school, they'd barely told her goodbye. She hadn't heard from them since. But she hadn't reached out to them, either. It was hard to want to stay in touch with people who'd never made a secret of what a burden you'd been to them from day one.

Instead, Emma had forged her own way in the world alone. Naturally, there hadn't been money for college, but she'd practically lived in the computer lab at school, learning everything she could about them. Her teacher Ms. Cabrera had been delighted to have such a keen student and had taken Emma under her wing to teach her even more than what she taught in the classroom. By the time Emma graduated from high school, she was an absolute whiz at all things computer-and-internet related—computer programming, computer systems, computer applications, computer security.

And, it went without saying, computer hacking. Not that Ms. Cabrera had taught Emma that. But the more she learned from her teacher, the more she figured out for herself. The more she figured out for herself, the more opportunities she had to learn other stuff. With knowledge came power. And shady online connections. And with shady online connections came even more knowledge—mostly about stuff that was in no way legal—followed by even more power.

But she'd used her powers for good instead of evil, eventually hanging out her shingle as a computer-security pro after wandering around doing odd jobs for a number of years. Her first clients had been individuals she found by advertising her skills online for a very fair price. Okay, she admitted she'd undercut other professionals. She'd needed to eat. And yes, okay, at that point, she'd been too self-absorbed to care that she was putting others out of business. She knew better now. Then word had gotten around to some local businesses, and that was where her income really started to blossom. It took a while for her to be able to make a good living, but ultimately it was an excellent living. Not to mention the perfect job for her. No one had any inkling they were dealing with a twenty-something, who'd never set foot on a university campus. She'd been smart enough, and savvy enough, for them to make assumptions about her that she just never bothered to correct.

Really, now that she thought about it, working as

Emma Brown, housekeeper, wasn't the first time she'd posed fraudulently. As Amber Finch, she'd cultivated a whole persona of smart, experienced—mature— computer expert. No, she'd never actively lied about her age or credentials—or lack of both. She'd set up her business and her online presence without ever having to deal with anyone in person. And no one had ever specifically asked for her age or credentials. Her employment had come almost exclusively by word of mouth and based on the reputation she earned for herself. If people had wanted to assume she was a multi-degreed, long-lived expert, then who was she to stop them?

Okay, okay, maybe she wasn't exactly the most honest person in the world—then or now. So sue her. Amber Finch had lacked a lot of desirable people skills—because she'd never been taught any desirable people skills. After she left home, she'd done what she had to do to get by in a world that didn't exactly help her along. Emma Brown was doing that, too. Neither of them had actively cheated anyone, and neither had ever consciously done any harm. She figured that made her better and more respectable than a lot of people. She'd earned her first paycheck from Summerlight through work that was honest, even if she wasn't. If she wanted to treat herself for the former instead of the latter, she would.

So when she strode out of Sudbury Community Bank that sunny mid-June afternoon, Emma turned right to head back to the restaurant where she had lunch on her first day in town two weeks ago. Jack's, she remembered it was called when she came upon it a second time. The place where Pax Lightfoot had invited her to join him for lunch shortly after they met, she likewise remembered immediately after.

But there was little chance she'd see him at Jack's this afternoon. He hadn't returned to the inn once since the day she met him, something she told herself she was extremely happy about. Even if there was a weird part of her that kind of missed him. Which made no sense. The two of them had barely spoken and spent maybe fifteen minutes together—if that. Not to mention he was the last person she should be interacting with anyway. Even putting aside his computer background—which she absolutely could not afford to do—Emma had no business missing any guy. She wasn't even sure how long she'd be able to stay in Sudbury. Hopefully for a while, but she would never be safe as long as Travis Swope's stupid bounty was still out there hanging over her head. Any day, some skeezy guy could look at her long enough and hard enough to recognize her as Amber Finch and out her again. Or, worse, grab her and throw her into the trunk of his car to make the cross-country trip to Las Vegas and Travis Swope. Hell, that skeezy guy could end up being Pax Lightfoot. So there would be no missing him. Period.

"Well, hello there," Marge the waitress said to Emma with a smile when she entered. "Long time no see."

Emma smiled back. "Hi. Yeah, I've been working at my new job."

"And how are Haven and Bennett treating you?"

"Great," Emma told her. "I really like it there."

Marge nodded. "They're good people. Injecting a lot of life into this sleepy old town. This little village used to be full of life once upon a time, and, thanks to them, it might just find its way back to being the happy, bustling place it used to be."

Emma couldn't help thinking she and Sudbury had a lot in common. She hoped she would find her way back to being happy and bustling before long.

"Got a free table?" she asked Marge.

"For you, doll, always." She swept a hand toward a dining room that was nearly empty, thanks to it being well past the lunch hour. "Take your pick."

"Thanks."

Emma chose a table by the window, where she could look at Sudbury on the other side and marvel again at its quaintness. Marge brought her a menu and a glass of water with a slice of lemon, then asked about how the inn was coming along and whether Haven and Bennett were still on target for a November opening. Emma replied with enthusiasm and affection for both the position and place, surprising herself at how genuinely delighted she was to be there. Then she ordered the pineapple-almond chicken salad and an iced tea and returned the menu to Marge. The waitress departed, leaving Emma to herself. Herself and the picturesque town beyond the restaurant windows.

Truly, Sudbury was adorable. Across the street from Jack's was a pub called the Bitter End and a café called Dragonfly, where, Emma couldn't help thinking, Litha Firefly would have felt right at home. Next door to Jack's on either side, she'd noticed as she strode from the bank, was a bookstore called Turn the Page and a coffee shop called the Magic Bean. The town was enchanting enough to be a set created for a streaming rom-com.

As if to make that enchantment reality, Pax Lightfoot suddenly stepped into it by stepping out of Dragonfly Café across the street. He was holding a paper bag and cup in one hand while he consulted his phone about something with the other. Unbidden, an odd warmth erupted in Emma's belly, spreading into her chest and pooling around her heart. Where it came from, she had no idea. She only knew that she liked the feeling. A lot. It had been a long time since she'd felt anything warm or sweet. It was just too bad that the cause of it now happened to be something—someone—she really shouldn't be feeling warm or sweet toward.

All that separated them was a narrow, barely two-lane street, so it was easy for her to watch him from the window. Today he was dressed in a different pair of baggy khakis and a different camp shirt, this one pale blue and spattered with a design she couldn't make out from where she sat, though something told her it would be just as whimsical as the parrots and mai tais on the one he'd been wearing two weeks ago. He'd seen a barber since she last encountered him, too, as his dark hair and beard were both cropped noticeably shorter.

Marge returned with her iced tea and salad then, so Emma looked away from the window to thank her and exchange a few more words. When she looked back out the window again, Pax was still standing in front of the café, holding his bag and cup and phone. But he wasn't looking at his phone anymore. He was looking at Emma. The motions of her interaction with Marge must have caught his attention, even from across the street.

He tucked his phone into the pocket of his pants, then lifted a hand in greeting. Although Emma told herself not to do anything that might be construed as inviting—like, say, waving back—she lifted her hand to him in return. And although she told herself to absolutely not smile—because smiles were, by nature, inviting gestures—she then smiled at him. *Dammit.* She couldn't help herself. There was just something about Pax Lightfoot, even from a distance, that made her smile.

And yep, it must have been inviting, because he immediately looked left and right up the street, then jogged across it, heading for Jack's. Without much realizing it—and without thinking about why she was doing it once she realized she was—she smoothed a hand over the pale yellow shirt she'd left untucked over her pastel floral skirt and then smoothed a hand over the sandy hair she'd left unbound to fall to her shoulders. The bell above Jack's front door jingled merrily as Pax entered, and the next thing she knew, he was standing by her table.

Clearly still not recognizing her as Amber Finch. Because he was smiling at her, not glaring at her and calling her some of the unspeakable names she'd been called for months as he pulled out his phone to dial his cult leader and turn her in.

"Hi," he said a little breathlessly. Which must have

been a result of his sprint across the street, because why else would he be breathless?

"Hi," Emma replied, feeling a little breathless herself at seeing him again, looking so gorgeous and sexy and sweet and appealing and…

Oh. That was why. In a word, *Uh-oh.*

"What brings you into town?" he asked.

"My day off," she told him. "And to cash my first paycheck."

He nodded once. "Congrats."

"Thanks."

They studied each other in silence for a moment. Emma held her breath as he looked at her, every cell in her body ready to bolt if he suddenly recognized her as Amber Finch. But he never offered a single indication that she was familiar to him in any other way than as Summerlight's new housekeeper whom he met a couple of weeks ago. In fact, he never stopped smiling. Unable to help herself, she smiled back.

For the past two weeks, she'd thought maybe the reason Pax hadn't figured out who she was when they first met was because the lighting had been bad in Haven's office and not much better in the foyer. And also because she'd kept her distance and cut their time together short on both occasions. She'd promised herself that if she ever saw him again, she would make sure those conditions stayed the same. Bad lighting. Distance. No prolonged contact. But even in good light and up close this way, even exchanging the long look they were now, he didn't recognize her. He had no idea who she really was.

She told herself she shouldn't be surprised by that. When she'd first adopted her new, more natural look, she'd barely recognized herself in the mirror. But she couldn't afford to trust in those physical changes alone to keep her safe. More than one of Travis Swope's groupies had seen something in her while she'd thought she was well disguised, something that had alerted him to her true identity and made him at least wonder if she was that girl everyone online was looking for. More than once, she'd had to literally run again and find somewhere else to hide. She was tired of hiding. Tired of running. She loved it here in Sudbury. She wanted to stay as long as she could.

She knew it was a bad idea to invite Pax to join her, even if he didn't recognize her, and even if it was the polite thing to do. Then she noted again the bag and cup in his hand. He already had his lunch. There was no reason for him to accept her invitation. She could ask him to sit down, and he would politely decline, then they could exchange a few more words, and he would be on his way, never suspecting she was anyone other than who she claimed to be: Emma Brown, housekeeper.

Easy peasy.

"Do you want to join me?" she asked.

It took all of a nanosecond for him to claim the seat opposite her. "Don't mind if I do."

Well. That hadn't worked out the way she'd planned. Funny, though, how she kind of didn't mind seeing her plan blow up in her face.

He really was very attractive. His dark eyes were alight with laughter behind his tortoiseshell glasses, and a small gold hoop she hadn't noticed before winked in one ear. His shirt collar was open enough that she could see part of a tattoo along his left collarbone, something that looked like writing, but not enough to read exactly what it was. All she could see was the first word, *Down*, followed by another that started with *th*. The pattern on his shirt that she hadn't been able to detect from across the street was comprised of retro-looking surfboards. She wondered if he had anything in his wardrobe that wasn't whimsical. Surely he dressed more conservatively to teach at Cornell. Or not. Something told her this was pretty standard attire for him.

She nodded toward the bag and cup he set on the table beside himself. "Looks like you already have lunch plans."

He looked at his purchases, too. "What this? Nah. It's actually tomorrow's breakfast." To illustrate that, he opened the bag and gave her a peek inside. Two scones that looked to be blueberry in nature. Then he lifted the cup, which contained coffee, she could tell, now that it was within smelling distance. "And this is just my usual three-p.m. pick-me-up. Which I needed at two p.m. today," he added with a grin. "I had to drive up to Summerlight to give Haven some flyers she needed for a mailing. Decided I'd grab some caffeine before getting back on the road."

She wondered why he'd made a one-hour drive one-way to give something to Haven that he could have dropped into the mail instead. Or even emailed so that she could print them up herself. Maybe he just liked Sudbury as much as she did and wanted to visit often.

As if to put a fine point on the thought, Marge returned and greeted Pax like an old friend as she set a glass of water in front of him. After ordering the Italian sub and fries with sour cream on the side, he told the server to put both their meals on one check and give it to him.

After Marge left, Emma mock-frowned at him. Well, sort of mock-frowned. She really didn't want him covering the bill. "You don't have to buy me lunch," she told him a little more crisply than she'd intended—and maybe a little more crisply than was necessary. "I can pay my own way. And I wanted to treat myself today. To celebrate earning my first paycheck."

He arched his brows in surprise at her vehemence. "I never said you couldn't pay your way. And fine, lunch is on you, then."

"*My* lunch is on me," she clarified for him.

Again, maybe a little too crisply. As much as she would have liked to pay for his, too, especially since she realized she was maybe being a little too stringent with the whole *I can take care of myself* thing—more of the old, mouthy, graceless Amber raising her head to make things difficult—she really needed to hang on to whatever cash she could in case she needed to beat a hasty retreat after he recognized her.

She winced. *Please don't recognize me*, she told him mentally. *Or, if you do, please be a decent guy and not some psycho Travis Swope sycophant.*

Before she could apologize or explain her behavior—not that she had any idea how to explain that without incriminating herself—Pax lifted his hands in surrender and said, defensively, "Okay, fine. We'll split the bill." The laughter was gone from his eyes now, to be replaced with concern. "I'm sorry. I didn't mean to offend you."

Damn. She really had gone too long without any kind of polite social interaction. Not that her social interactions had ever been that polite to begin with. Over the years after leaving home, she'd pretty much veered off the path of civility and onto the highway of snark. By that time, she'd spent her entire life living in deference to her parents. She'd been as quiet as she could be so that she never disturbed them. She'd done everything she could to make herself small and unnoticed. She'd stayed in her room reading, she'd never made waves at school or anywhere else and she'd certainly never talked back, even when her parents were telling her what a burden she was. She had done her best to stay invisible the whole time she was growing up.

Leaving that environment had been so liberating for her. Once it had finally occurred to her that she no longer had to be that quiet little mouse, she'd swung fully to the opposite side of the pendulum. She'd started dressing in wildly colorful and outrageous clothing that commanded notice, then paired them with cosmetics that were every bit as splashy. She'd even started vlogging about both, something that directed even more attention her way.

And when she'd finally found her voice, it had been *loud*. She'd begun speaking up and speaking her mind, and damn anyone who didn't want to hear it. Then, when she started making her living in the male-dominated

world of tech, she'd leveled up her in-your-face auda-
ciousness to the nth power. A woman in tech had to give
as good as she got, right out of the gate. She had to give
better than she got, even. The minute she showed any
kind of softness or deference, the men outnumbering
her swooped in to swallow her whole. Amber Finch had
made herself one of the noisiest, flashiest, most snide
creatures on the planet to make sure she never slipped
into invisibility again.

At least until that loud, splashy snideness turned the
world where she lived against her.

But Pax wasn't trying to swallow her whole, and he
was seeing her just fine. He didn't want to make her
feel small. He was only trying to be nice. It had been
so long since she'd experienced niceness from anyone
that she'd forgotten it even existed. Hundreds upon hundreds of death threats—and worse—could make a person a tad wary.

"You didn't offend me," she told him more calmly.
"I'm sorry. I'm just not used to—" *What?* she wondered.
*Not used to being treated kindly by a guy? Not used to
being treated kindly by anyone?* She sighed and tried
again. "I'm sorry," she repeated simply. "I didn't mean
it like that."

He looked as if he wanted to ask her what she had
meant, but, thankfully, he let it go. He smiled again,
and even if it didn't quite reach his eyes this time, his
good humor returned.

"It's okay," he told her. "Let's just start over." He
stuck out a hand. "Hi. I'm Pax Lightfoot. Assistant pro-

fessor of computer science, writer of tech articles and social media professional."

She hesitated, then extended her hand across the table to take his, trying not to notice the little buzz of exuberance that accompanied the gesture. "Emma Brown, housekeeper," she told him.

"Emma Brown," he repeated, slowly and melodically, as if he were uttering a magical incantation. "It's nice to meet you."

For some reason, he didn't release her hand after the greeting. For some reason, she didn't release his, either. For a moment, they only gazed at each other in silence. Somehow, she thought it was not so much because neither knew what to say, but because each was kind of sizing the other up.

And still, he didn't recognize her.

Marge returned with his sandwich, and he finally let go of Emma's hand. He let go of *her*, she couldn't help noticing. Not the other way around. Usually she was the one who let go first. She liked to be the one in control of her interactions with others. That was another way she'd survived in tech. But with Pax, who was even a tech guy, she'd let him be the one to end their contact first.

She wasn't sure how to interpret that. So she decided to think about it later.

"So tell me about yourself, Emma Brown," he said as he dipped a french fry into his sour cream.

Instead of doing as he requested, she curled up her lip at his actions. "Sour cream on fries?" she asked.

He halted with a white-tipped fry halfway to his

mouth. "Sure. It's delicious. People put sour cream on baked potatoes all the time. Turns out, it's good on fries, too."

She couldn't argue with his logic. But she also didn't want to ever dip her fries into sour cream.

"What do you dip your fries in?" he asked.

"Sriracha. Duh."

He chuckled. "Heathen." He popped the fry into his mouth, savored it as if it were the food of the gods, then repeated, "So tell me about yourself, Emma Brown. Other than the sriracha thing."

Oh, she really wished she had been the one first on the draw with that question. She did not want to tell Pax Lightfoot anything about herself. At all. Naturally, she didn't want him to know about Amber Finch. But she didn't want to sit here and lie to him about being Emma Brown, either. Even if she had memorized every last detail of Emma Brown's life that she had found online in case a conversation like this ever came up. Even if she had lied to plenty of other people over the last nine months without a second thought or a single regret. Even if there was no danger of Pax finding out later that she'd lied to him if he went to look her up, since Emma Brown of Altoona now looked like Amber Finch. To any outside observer, she truly was Emma Brown. Even if she wasn't, you know, Emma Brown.

"There's not much to tell," she said. Great. Lying right off the bat. Were she to indeed talk about herself as Amber Finch, she could tell him a tale that rivaled the greatest Greek tragedies.

"I know you're from Altoona," he told her. "Home of a bunch of stuff I don't remember now."

"Hedda Hopper and the original horseshoe curve. It's also the birthplace of Georgism and is sister city to St. Pölten, Austria." She recited it all dutifully, as she had on the handful of occasions when the need had arisen. She'd memorized everything she could about Altoona, too.

"Right," he said. "Now I know more about Altoona than I do about Emma Brown."

Okay, fine. She'd tell him all about Emma Brown of Altoona, Pennsylvania. She'd even be honest about it. Just not in the way Pax thought.

"So you want to know about Emma Brown," she began, replaying every internet mention of her stolen identity in her mind as she got it all lined up. "Let's see now. She grew up in a trailer park in the burbs, attended North Drayton K through eight and graduated from Crestwood High School. When she was twelve, she won a red ribbon for her Pfeffernüsse cookies at the Blair County Fair. Junior division, but a ribbon just the same. She broke her elbow playing field hockey in eighth grade, and she was nominated for homecoming queen her sophomore year in high school. Unfortunately, she only made it to third runner-up. She was a hospital volunteer alongside her aunt Sissy the whole time she was in high school. Her birthday is May twenty-fifth, making her a Gemini. She's twenty-seven years old. There. Now you know everything I do about Emma Brown."

And she hadn't lied once. *Woo. Hoo.*

In actuality, Emma would turn thirty in late October,

making her a Scorpio. And the closest she'd ever been to a homecoming court was looking out the library window at the football field one afternoon when they were practicing how it was all going to go down at halftime that night. She'd never baked a cookie—or anything else—in her entire life. And hospital volunteer? Forget about it. Hospitals gave her a major wiggins. The trailer-park part did sort of skirt the truth. Emma's parents' house had been next door to a trailer park, and her best friend, Tanya, had lived in one of those trailers until she and her family moved away when the two of them were both nine, leaving Emma without a bestie for, well, ever. But the rest of it…

None of it could have been further from the truth.

Pax had smiled the entire time she was talking, and when he met her gaze again, there was a maybe-maybe-not suspicious look in his dark eyes. "Not quite, I don't," he told her. "There's a lot more to you than you're letting on."

Something hot and frantic exploded in Emma's belly at the comment. In spite of his apparent levity, she was terrified he was about to accuse her of being Amber Finch.

"What else could there possibly be to know about me?" she replied cautiously.

Maybe a little too cautiously. He seemed to sense her alarm, because his dark brows knit downward.

"What kind of music do you like?" he asked. "Books? Movies? What are your hobbies? What's your favorite color? If you could be any animal in the world, what would you be?"

The heat in her belly slowly evaporated. Oh. Okay. She could answer those questions. Truthfully again, too, since she had no idea how the real Emma Brown might have responded, so she would just go with her own likes and dislikes for the responses.

"I like all kinds of music," she said. Honestly. "Alternative and punk best, I guess, but I'll listen to pretty much anything. For books, mostly fantasy and historical fiction, but I read across the board. For movies, fantasy again and action. A few thrillers. I don't really have a lot of hobbies." Not outside of coding and hacking and gaming, but no way was she going to tell him that, since that cut *too* close to home. "My favorite color is purple. And for an animal, I'd be…" She was about to tell him she would be a firefly if she could, since that was her favorite. But she couldn't risk him making the connection to Litha Firefly, however unlikely that seemed. So she went with her second favorite instead. "A beluga whale, I think," she said.

That last reply halted another french fry on its way to Pax's mouth. "Beluga whale? That's an interesting choice."

She shrugged. "Belugas are nice. They seem happy. They smile a lot. And they never hurt anybody."

He thought about that for a second, then nodded. "I can see that," he said before popping the fry into his mouth.

She wasn't sure if he was saying he could see that about belugas or about her. Either way, though, his words made her feel good. Before she could feel too good, though, and before he could ask her more things,

things that she might have to think about a lot before replying so she wouldn't have to lie, she turned the conversation to him.

"How about you?" she asked. "What are all your favorites? What are your hobbies? What animal would you be?"

He munched for a thoughtful minute, sipped his water, then answered the questions he'd asked her, in the order that they'd been issued. "Jazz is definitely my favorite music. Especially old jazz. Ella Fitzgerald was…" He shook his head in awe, then sent a chef's kiss skyward. "She's transcendent. For books, my favorite writers are Faulkner and Hemingway, with Dashiell Hammett and Raymond Chandler a close second. Movies—definitely anything film noir, though I love pretty much anything in black and white and have a soft spot for screwball comedies."

"I'm sensing a pattern here," Emma said after digesting all he said. Now she was smiling, too. "You're actually a ninety-eight-year-old man, aren't you, Pax?"

He laughed at that. "No, I just like old stuff—that's all. A lot."

Someday she would ask him why that was, but she could tell he was already thinking about the other questions. Emma had just enough time to marvel at how she was thinking about him in terms of *someday*, since she'd rarely thought of any guy that way, even ones she'd dated for months, when he started talking again.

"My only real hobby is gaming, I guess—playing, not designing. And I've kind of started dabbling in home brewing beer, but I haven't gotten very far with it. Sanitation can be a real challenge. My favorite color is probably blue. And if I could be any animal, I'd like to be a pangolin."

She couldn't hide her surprise at that last. "A pangolin? That's kind of…exotic. That's even more exotic than a beluga whale."

"Pangolins are cool animals," he said. "They seem like pushovers—they're toothless and defenseless, and they look like some kid's favorite plushie. But they have such a tough exterior that predators can almost never take them out. Sharp scales on their tails, too. They're just bad mamma jammas—that's all. They do their own thing, but if someone tries to mess with them, they can take care of themselves just fine."

If there were ever a more telling comment uttered by anyone, Emma had never heard it. As amiable and affable as Pax Lightfoot seemed, there was something inside him that was anything but. At some point in his life—probably when he was a child, since that was usually when the stuff that really defined people happened—he'd felt defenseless enough to have to grow armor. He wanted to be left alone, but if not, he could be a bad mamma jamma. Emma could totally relate. Someday she'd ask him about that, too.

Someday.

Instead of focusing on that now, however, she told him, "Home brewing sounds interesting."

Not that that was the only thing about Pax that sounded interesting. The more she learned about him, the better she liked him. Which meant she needed to stop learning about him ASAP.

In spite of that, there were a million more questions she wanted to ask him. How had he grown up? He'd told her nothing about his past except that his parents were liars and he was not in contact with them, something that only made her more curious about his past. And somehow she sensed the lack of details following such a bombshell revelation had been deliberate on his part. She should just ask him point-blank what his life had been like growing up. But after the pangolin comment, she was reluctant to pry. And it wasn't like she wanted to risk having him ask about her own childhood.

Not to mention you don't want to learn any more about him than you already have, she reminded herself. Right? Right. Best to remember that.

They spent the rest of their lunch talking about other things, such as how Dragonfly Café made killer scones and the Magic Bean's espresso could keep a person going for days. About Summerlight's past history of feuding families and its current rehabilitation. About how much Sudbury itself was changing in the wake of the mansion's revitalization. After Marge cleared away their empty plates and brought their—separate— checks, they paid for their meals and headed for the exit.

The moment they were through the door, however, they seemed to run out of things to say. As their silence grew, so did their awkwardness. Their gazes met long enough to ricochet off each other again, Emma looking up one side of the street, Pax looking down the other. It was another beautiful summer day, which every day in Sudbury seemed to be. The sky was clear blue, and a docile breeze stirred the hem of Emma's skirt. But she might as well have been standing at the bottom of a dank, dark well, so isolated did she suddenly feel.

She looked at Pax again, at the silky beard her fingers itched to stroke and the dark eyes she could drown in if she wasn't careful. At the tattooed letters inked below his elegant collarbone—she could make out the second word now, so the phrase began with *Down these*, but the rest of whatever it said disappeared beneath the fabric of his shirt—as did the broad shoulders straining against the garment. At the full mouth, half curled into a flirty smile, that she suddenly wanted to stand up on tiptoe to kiss. She had to curl her fingers into fists at her sides to keep from touching him. Because in that moment, all she wanted to do was touch Pax. And kiss Pax. And wake up in the morning beside Pax. It had just been so long since she had shared any kind of closeness with anyone—personal or physical. And now a man who looked like a paladin from one of her favorite novels, a man filled with warmth and wit and good will, a man who was so much—*dayum*—so much sexier than any guy she had ever encountered…

Where was she? She was starting to feel a little dizzy. Oh, yeah. Now she remembered. She was feeling lonely and needy and wanting to touch and kiss and make love with Pax. Right.

Wrong! she immediately corrected herself. There would be no doing any of those things!

She curled her fists tighter. "Um, it was nice seeing you again," she said in an effort to dispel both her thoughts and the cumbersome quiet. "Thank you for lunch."

"I didn't pay for your lunch," he reminded her.

She smiled. "I know. Thank you."

He smiled back. But there was still an odd distance between them for some reason. As if they'd both felt safe as long as they were inside the restaurant, but now that they were out in the big, wide world again, neither felt quite comfortable.

"Can I give you a lift back to Summerlight?" he asked.

As much as she would have liked to say yes, she shook her head. She really shouldn't spend any more time with him than she already had. Especially with the sudden sexy-time feelings that were coming at her out of nowhere. As nice as the afternoon with Pax had been—in fact, it was because of how nice the afternoon with him had been—she couldn't afford to get any closer to him than she already was. He really was a good guy. She hadn't met very many of those in her life. The way the last nine months had gone, she'd begun to wonder if there were even any good guys left out there. Actual good guys, she meant, not the ones who called themselves *Nice Guys* but were really woman-hating mouth breathers.

"That's okay," she finally told him. "Thanks. It's such a nice day, and I could use the walk."

He nodded. "It has been a nice day, hasn't it?"

Too nice, she wanted to say. *Dangerously nice.*

So she only told him, "Thanks again. Guess I'll see you when I see you."

He nodded and lifted a hand, then headed back across the street to where he'd parked his car. Emma watched him go, waving again as he lifted a hand when he drove off.

I'll see him when I see him, she thought, echoing her words to him. Part of her hoped like hell that was months—even years—away. She really couldn't afford to get too close to Pax. He very well could be a member of Travis Swope's tribe. And even if he wasn't—which, okay, he probably wasn't, because he was way too decent to be of that ilk—he had to know about the six-figure bounty on Amber Finch's head. There was no way he could make his living on the internet and not know about it. And six figures was a life-changing amount of money. Even the most decent person in the world could be swayed by that under the right circumstances.

But there was another part of Emma that hoped Pax had a reason to come back to Summerlight very soon. And as much as she told that part of herself to cool it, that her life was way too complicated right now to get close to anyone, for any reason, she could tell that part of her didn't want to listen. It had just been so long since she'd had any kind of interaction with a person that wasn't, at best, superficial and, at worst, dangerous. It had felt good today, just talking to someone. Laughing with someone. Being close to someone. She was only now beginning to realize how very lonely she had been for the better part of a year.

And maybe if for no other reason than that, she needed to keep Pax at arm's length. It would be too easy to fall for him, and she could fall for all the wrong reasons. Loneliness sucked. But until she knew she could trust again, lonely had to be how she remained.

Chapter Four

Pax could count on one hand how many times he'd visited Summerlight since the beginning of the year, prior to Emma Brown's arrival. He was going to be breaking that record before the month of June was even over. Only a few days after running into her in Sudbury and sharing what had been, without question, the nicest afternoon he'd ever had, he was headed back to the inn again. Not because he wanted to see her, but because he had some documents that needed Haven and Bennett's physical signatures. Sure, he could have just dropped them into the mail and waited for their return. They weren't time sensitive or anything. But who trusted the US mail system these days? Other than everyone who'd ever used it, because the US mail system was totally trustworthy? You could never be too careful, and—

And okay, okay. He wanted to see Emma, too. It wasn't that far a drive from Ithaca. Hell, when he'd done his undergraduate degree in Chicago, he'd had to live so far out of the city to make it affordable that it had taken him nearly an hour to get to class every morning. And he hadn't had Emma waiting for him at his destination, which was something that definitely made his current commute fly by.

Anyway.

It was late afternoon when he arrived, thanks to the Fundamental Programming Concepts class he was subbing in this week. He found Haven and Bennett on the patio in back of the inn, where she was setting up the grill and Bennett was making a pitcher of something almost certainly cocktail in nature. The first time Pax met Bennett, he and Haven were at odds over how the house they'd inherited together from his great-aunt last fall should be handled. To the point that they were barely speaking to each other, and Haven had referred to her now-fiancé exclusively as *the backstabbing SOB*. And Pax had to admit that his first impression of Bennett had been one of clichéd uptight businessman, all buttoned up and battened down and ready to blow a gasket. Now his hair was badly in need of a cut, he obviously hadn't shaved for days, his baggy shorts and loose T-shirt were streaked with dirt, and he was barefoot.

Haven had been such a good influence on him.

It might as well have been a Saturday, so at ease were they both, and so languid were the summer days every time Pax came to Summerlight. He knew the image was deceiving and that the couple was putting in more than full-time hours to get the inn up and running in time for its opening. But sometimes you had to take a weekday and remind yourself to enjoy life.

As if to illustrate that very thing, after greeting him, Bennett held up the pitcher and asked, "Negroni?" Then he said, "It's five o'clock somewhere," citing the universal excuse for cocktails.

"Thanks, but no," Pax told him. "I can't stay that long. Just brought up the contract rider for you guys to sign. And it's a bit of a drive back, so no alcohol."

"Just toss it onto the table," Haven told him. "We'll go over it tomorrow and, if everything's good, sign off on it. We should be able to get it back to you by the weekend."

"Thanks," he said, placing the folder on the table. "But don't worry about mailing them. I can come back and pick them up."

Haven gave him that smile again—the one she'd used that first day, when he asked so many questions about Emma. Was he really that obvious?

He looked away from Haven, glancing around the grounds and patio, telling himself it wasn't because he was looking for Emma but to assess the progress of the house. As always, the mansion glittered like a magnificent gem in the long, slanting sunlight. And he wondered where Emma was.

"How are things in Ithaca?" Haven asked him.

"Good," he told her.

"How's Joel Cairo?"

Joel Cairo was Pax's cat, a big black Tom who'd shown up in his backyard a couple winters ago, skinny and sneezing, with ice-encrusted paws. These days, Cairo spent most of his time in a sunny living room window plotting the demise of the red-bellied woodpecker that lived in the sycamore tree out front. A demise that would never come, since Cairo had shown zero interest in setting foot outside the house once he entered it and made himself at home.

"Cairo is great," he told Haven. "Still enjoying the treats you sent for his Gotcha Day."

"I always wanted a cat," she told him. "But my mom was allergic, and I never lived in any apartment buildings that allowed pets. Once Summerlight is up and running, Bennett and I are going to adopt a couple. Aren't we, Bennett?"

Bennett stopped stirring long enough to look at her. "Wait, what? We're getting a cat?"

But Haven had already moved on to a new topic. "I've been thinking about the video you mentioned doing for Summerlight that you could post online," she told Pax.

That was good. Because Pax had practically forgotten about that himself, so full had his head been of Emma. Although he was in the process of making a full-length online tour of the inn once it was up, he wanted to tease it in advance with interesting little snippets here and there of variously themed topics in the meantime. Keep the interest he'd generated with the crowdfunding campaign last fall, which was ongoing until the inn's opening this fall. But Haven knew better than he did what would interest people most. He was open to any ideas she had.

"What kind of thinking?" he asked her.

"I've been taking snippets of video here and there of all the improvements we've been doing since Christmas," she told him. "And I have some footage from even before that that I took when we first moved in to send to my mom to show her what kind a deplorable state a lot of the house was in. And I have new footage of what it looks like now that I've been sending her to show her how far we've come. I was thinking maybe we could mix and match it."

"So, like, before and after?" Pax asked. "A progress mashup-type thing?"

Haven nodded. "To show how far this place has come."

"That could be very cool," he said.

The rehab of the house was what had brought in so much money on the crowdfunding site in the first place. Pax had convinced a lot of DIY influencers and historic-home enthusiasts to post the campaign to save Summerlight for their followers, something that ended up getting millions of hits and generating even more dollars. "I could do two-or-three-minute pieces for people to watch when they're taking breaks," he said with a smile. "And then for them to share to their own social media for others to see and also share on *their* social media."

Oh, how Pax loved creating viral sensations. It was the bread and butter of businesses like Summerlight.

"Oh, yay, you think it's a good idea," Haven said with a grin. "I'm never sure with some of them that pop into my head."

Bennett laughed. "Yeah, the one about building a water slide from the roof to the lake wasn't so hot."

"Only because of the potential liability problems."

"And the architectural ones."

"I could've made it happen," she assured him.

"I know you could. But I think our efforts—and funds—are better served with more, uh, traditional attractions."

That got Haven talking again about the nature hikes she wanted to put together. As she spoke, Bennett poured her and himself a Negroni and filled a glass with sparkling water for Pax. He was just lifting it to his lips when Emma strode out of the inn to join them. The sun had dropped low enough to once again bathe her in gold, giving her that impression of some kind of heavenly being. Her hair was caught at her nape in a ponytail, but the wind picked up her long bangs and danced with them. She was wearing a lavender T-shirt over the same skirt she'd had on every time he'd seen her.

Clearly, she didn't have an extensive wardrobe, something he both admired and wondered about. It was great that she wasn't a conspicuous consumer. But it was concerning that she seemed to consume almost nothing at all. Maybe it was just her favorite skirt.

"We're grilling tonight, if you're interested, Emma," Haven announced. "Bennett's making... What are you making again, Bennett?"

"Chicken caprese," he said. "With tomatoes and basil from the garden. And a nice pasta al limone on the side."

"In that case, I'm definitely interested," Emma replied.

"I'm going to slice the bread," Haven offered brightly, clearly not wanting to be left out.

"I'll slice the bread," Bennett corrected her. "You nearly lost a thumb last time you did it."

Emma frowned. "Oh, yeah. Okay, you can slice the bread."

Pax chuckled. It was no secret to anyone in Sudbury—or probably on Staten Island, where she grew up—that Haven was absolutely useless in a kitchen. Unless it was to completely remodel it.

At the sound of his laughter, Emma glanced over, seeing him for the first time. She smiled, and he wasn't sure, but she might have blushed a little.

"Oh, hi, Pax," she said.

"Hey, Emma."

"Unfortunately Pax can't stay for dinner," Haven said. "He has to be heading back to Ithaca in—"

"You know what?" Pax interjected before she could finish. "I could probably stay for dinner after all. I was going to have to pick up something in Sudbury before driving back anyway."

That he'd hoped he would run into Emma between now and then and ask her to join him for dinner at the restaurant instead of taking it to go was neither here nor there. They could eat anywhere. As long as they were in the same place.

"Gosh, what a shocker," Haven said.

Yeah, yeah, yeah.

Emma made her way to the patio proper, and the two couples—*Not that you and Emma are a couple*, Pax hastily corrected himself when the thought materialized—enjoyed what would become a very nice evening of dinner and conversation. All of the latter surrounded the goings-on at Summerlight, current events in the news, Sudbury gossip, and the latest summer blockbusters playing weekly at the village's sole movie theater. Not one peep about anything personal, so Pax knew no more about Emma by the time dinner concluded than he had when it began. Except that she really didn't like super-hero franchises and thought old Mrs. Hanover in town should absolutely *not* be giving that much money to her ne'er-do-well nephew, Andy.

Which Pax totally agreed with. Not so much the part about superhero franchises, since he had enjoyed the Captain America movies a lot. But Andy Hanover re-ally was a creep. As far as Pax was concerned, there was a special place in hell for anyone who preyed upon the elderly. Unfortunately, a good chunk of that popu-lation were members of his estranged family.

Since Haven and Bennett had provided dinner, Pax and Emma took care of cleaning up in the kitchen, after which point there was really no reason for him to hang around. Well, none other than that he just really wanted to hang around. He only wished he could figure out an excuse to make that happen.

Haven and Bennett had returned to the patio, and Pax was about to reluctantly voice his intention to leave, when Emma slapped a hand against her forehead and said, "Crap."

"What's wrong?" he asked.

"Haven had me clean out a closet full of stuff today that I now need to take down to the boathouse. Two big boxes. I totally forgot about them when I saw you out on the—"

She clammed up before finishing, tight enough that her lips nearly disappeared. A ribbon of something warm and pleasant unwound inside Pax to realize he'd made her forget to do her job.

"Anyway," she hurried on, "Haven's using the boathouse for storage until she has a chance to go through stuff, and I need to take the boxes down there."

"Where are they?" he asked. "I'll help you carry them down." It was the least he could do for being so distracting.

"You don't have to," she objected. "I know you have a long drive home. And it's going to be dark soon."

"It's not that far a drive," he told her. "And it's not that dark yet. It'll just take a minute."

"Thanks," she told him. "I appreciate it. Then we can both finally call it a day."

It actually took more than a minute, and when they eventually got everything down to the boathouse, Pax realized he didn't want to call it a day. As gorgeous as the view of the lake was from the mansion and the patio, it was incredible here on the waterfront. The moon had crept over the horizon, full and bright, but still hung low enough to spill a faint pearly trail across the lake. The sky around it was smudged with lavenders, pinks, and golds, but it wasn't dark enough yet for any stars to brave an appearance. Two sailboats were silhouetted near the middle of the lake, and as he watched, a pair of loons flew by to nestle in a nearby marsh.

He really had lived all over the place, in every kind of environment imaginable. Mountainous and coastal, temperate and tropical, wet and dry. Big cities, small towns, rural areas too tiny and separated from civilization to even be called civilization. He'd fallen asleep to the sounds of everything from police sirens to babbling brooks, and he'd watched the sun set and rise from more horizons that he could count. But he'd honestly never seen a night as beautiful as this one.

"It's nice, isn't it?" Emma said softly from behind him.

When he turned to look at her, it all began to make sense. This was why the evening was more beautiful than any other. Because Emma was standing in the middle of it.

"Yeah, it is," he agreed.

A short dock extended from the boathouse, and she strode down its entirety to bring herself to its edge. Pax was helpless not to follow her. The evening was silent save for the whisper of the wind in the trees, the lapping of the lake against the dock and the chirping of a chorus of crickets. For a long moment, neither of them spoke but instead only enjoyed the quiet serenity of their surroundings. When he finally looked over at Emma, it was to see that she had closed her eyes. As if she sensed him looking at her, however, she opened them again and met his gaze. Then, with a smile, she toed off her sandals and sat down on the dock's edge, dangling her feet above the water. Even though he knew he really should start heading home, there was no way he was going to sacrifice a chance to spend time with her in a place like this. So he took a seat beside her.

"I come down here a lot in the evenings," she told him. "My first few nights here, I had so much trouble sleeping. So I would just sit up in bed and look out my bedroom window and be amazed at how peaceful and quiet everything beyond it was."

The way she'd said she had trouble sleeping made Pax think that the reason for it wasn't typical insomnia. Like maybe she had other reasons for not being able to sleep. Like maybe troubling reasons. Like maybe reasons that weren't peaceful or quiet at all.

Then she added, almost absently, "It had been a while since I was able to do that anywhere. I'd kind of forgotten what peace and quiet could be like."

For the first time, it occurred to him to wonder just how Emma had ended up in Sudbury. This wasn't the kind of place—yet—to be a draw for anyone other than the folks who already lived here. Hell, according to Haven, a lot of people had been leaving Sudbury in the last few years, especially the young ones like him and Emma. Before Summerlight's renovation, there had been few jobs in town and not a lot of entertainment. Haven and Bennett hoped the whole village would eventually benefit from the inn's opening and become a tourist destination in and of itself, creating more jobs and more fun, and earning its residents new ways to make a living. For now, though, it was still just a sleepy little hamlet. One that never should have even been on the radar for someone like Emma. Just how the hell had she found her way here in the first place?

Amid the curious meanderings of his thoughts, she continued, "Then, one night, it occurred to me that I could actually be a part of that serenity if I wanted. All I had to do was take a few steps outside. I've just never lived anywhere as beautiful as this."

"No lakes in Altoona, huh?" he asked.

She shook her head. "It's on the eastern slopes of the Allegheny Mountains. *Altoona* is probably a corruption of a Cherokee word meaning *high lands of great worth*. The area was settled during the Revolutionary War to protect lead deposits in the hills. In the eighteen hundreds, they built a canal and had to use railroad cars to haul the barges up through it. So, yeah. No lakefronts like this."

There it was again. She was talking about her hometown as if she were a fifth grader reading aloud from a book report on the subject. Maybe she was just really proud of where she came from. It was still kind of… odd, the way she talked about it.

He wanted to ask her what had brought her to Sudbury. But he was starting to sense that whatever it was might not be a happy event and that it might require easing into. Instead, he asked, "So why did you leave Altoona? And where did you go when you left?"

For a moment, she looked a little troubled by the question. Or maybe it was just the way the falling daylight slanted across her face. She smiled, though, even if that, too, looked less than easy. But she didn't evade his questions, which, for some reason, he'd kind of thought she would do. She wasn't particularly specific, but she at least answered honestly, and for that he gave her props.

"I left home at eighteen," she told him. "My parents never had much money, so there was no way I could go to college, but I'd been working since I was fifteen, and I'd saved up enough money to strike out on my own. So I did."

The part about being poor didn't surprise him. He'd figured as much when she said she grew up in a trailer park. Not that there weren't some very nice mobile-home communities out there, but those were generally referred to as, you know, *mobile-home communities*. Trailer parks, on the other hand, were a whole 'nother animal. Maybe it was just a matter of semantics, but Pax had never heard anyone speak favorably of living in a *trailer park*. And the handful of times he'd lived in trailer parks with his family, they hadn't been nearly as nice as the mobile-home communities he'd seen elsewhere in his travels.

"Where did you go?" he asked again.

He waited for her to reply *Here and there*, as she had the first time they met, but she didn't. Well, not in those exact words.

"First thing I did was buy a beater car," she said. "Then I just started driving. I'd never left my home state before—I'd barely ever been out of my hometown—and I suddenly realized that I could go anywhere I wanted." She sighed with much contentment before adding, "It was so weird driving over the state line for the first time. Like I was committing some hugely rebellious act I'd get in big trouble for."

Pax couldn't imagine having parents who would care so much about their child that they worried about their safety. When he was a kid, his parents barely ever even knew where he was. Then he remembered how Emma said she was estranged from her folks. How they hadn't been close. So maybe the two of them had that in common, too.

Just to be sure, he asked, "Guess your mom and dad weren't too keen on you taking off on your own, huh?"

He wasn't prying—or at least, didn't mean to. He'd just never had anything that might be remotely considered a normal home or family life, and he was always genuinely interested to hear other people talk about their own. It gave him hope for the rest of the world, knowing it wasn't the norm for people to grow up surrounded by scoundrels and jackals, overlooked at best and manipulated at worst. He hoped that was something he and Emma didn't have in common.

Her gaze glanced off his at the question, settling on the water below their feet. He suddenly realized that maybe he'd been too hasty to assume she'd had a happy childhood, in spite of what she'd told him about it so far.

"Actually, I think they were pretty happy to be free of me," she said softly. "I mean, I know they were. I was one of those unplanned surprises who just made their already difficult lives even more difficult. Me taking off probably made them both sigh a big sigh of relief."

Oh, nicely done, Pax. Way to sink a beautiful evening right to the bottom of the lake.

He had no idea what to say in response to that. But Emma didn't seem to mind, because she kept talking.

"But it's okay," she said. "I'm okay. It was actually pretty freeing leaving home."

When she looked up at him again, she really did seem to be okay about what she was saying. "My parents never mistreated or abused me. They fed me and clothed me and made sure I got on the bus to school every morning. I think they thought that made them good parents. But they didn't talk to me unless they had to. They didn't help me with my homework or come up with fun crafts or play games or anything like that. We never did stuff as a family." She shrugged philosophically. "They took care of me, but they didn't love me. I'm not sure I even understood what that meant when I was a kid. It was just the way things were."

Pax hated that she was so matter-of-fact about that. Even if he did sympathize completely.

Now she looked up at the sky. "Leaving home was a good thing for me to do. The first thing I ever did in my life that made me happy. That was as weird a feeling as crossing the state line. I'd never really felt it before."

"So you just took off to see the world," he said.

"I did," she replied with surprising satisfaction. "As much of it as I could anyway. Which has so far been a surprising amount."

Haven had told Pax that all of Emma's work experience had been in Pennsylvania and the mid-Atlantic area. He wasn't sure he'd call a tour of a half dozen states, tops, a surprising amount of travel, but to someone who hadn't left her hometown for the first two-thirds of her life, he could see how it would be. He wondered what Emma would think about him if he told her the extent of his own travels.

"So what did you do after you left home?" he asked again, since she'd never really told him that part.

She sighed. "For a while, I just wandered around, seeing places I'd always promised myself I wanted to see. Places I'd read about in books or seen in movies. Hollywood and Vine in LA, Chinatown in San Francisco. Pikes Peak. Petrified Forest. The Las Vegas Strip. I was such a tourist those first few years."

Now Pax was confused. The trailer-park-girl not-quite-homecoming-queen cookie-baker from Altoona had driven thousands of miles from home in her beater car to go sightseeing? What, there wasn't enough on the East Coast to pique her interest?

"Wait a minute," he said. "I thought you'd never traveled west of Pennsylvania. But all those places are all literally the West."

Now she looked a little panicked again. "Who told you I never traveled west of Pennsylvania?"

Oops. Busted. "Haven might have mentioned it at some point."

He was afraid Emma would be mad that he'd been snooping around about her without her permission. Instead she seemed super uneasy and for a reason he couldn't identify.

But all she said was "Oh. Yeah. Well. I actually did go across country at one point after I left home. Spent some time on the West Coast. I've been in this area for the last bit of my life now. I guess I never mentioned the traveling to Haven."

So maybe the two of them really were equally well traveled. Yet another thing they had in common. And what the hell. In for a penny, in for a pound. She already knew he'd been asking Haven about her past. So he stayed on the subject.

"Haven says you have a pretty eclectic résumé, too. Waitress, bartender, salesclerk, cashier."

"Yeah, I was all those things at one point. It took me a while to figure out what I was good at," she told him.

Which seemed like an odd thing to say, since she was working as a housekeeper even though she had a degree in English from Dickinson, he remembered. How had that happened if there had been no money for college when she left home, and she'd spent time on the West Coast after leaving?

"So how and when did you finally end up at Dickinson?" he asked.

She met his gaze levelly, and this time she did seem a bit irritated. "Just how much did you and Haven talk about me? Did she just hand over my résumé?"

Pax supposed he couldn't blame her for being annoyed. It really hadn't been cool for him and Haven to have been talking about her behind her back that way. Even if he was still intensely curious about her, he dropped the subject. For now.

"Sorry," he said, genuinely apologetic. "I don't mean to pry."

"It's okay," she told him, relaxing some. "But Dickinson is a story for another time."

He supposed he should be grateful that she was at least thinking in terms of there being *another time* for them. And he was. Grateful, he meant. Although he was thinking in terms of *another time* as well.

Then she said, "Enough about me for now. It's your turn to spill your guts. So come on, Pax. I want to know everything there is to know about you." With that, his gratitude evaporated.

Chapter Five

As much as Pax loved hearing people talk about their own pasts and childhoods, he hated talking about his own. But what the hell. Emma had been honest with him all night, so the least he could do was be honest with her. "I wasn't close to my folks, either," he said. "And I left home even younger than you. I was seventeen when I took off."

She looked at him in clear concern, in spite of having done something similar herself. "Wow, your family didn't come looking for you? I mean, you being a minor and all?"

He shook his head. "It probably took them a couple of weeks to even notice I was gone. I come from a big family. A really big family. And we all traveled together all the time, and sometimes we kids switched up who we stayed with, aunt-and-uncle wise. Everyone probably figured I was staying with someone else or I was out wreaking havoc with my cousins and would come home in due time. It was a pretty fluid situation."

"Sounds like you moved around a lot as a kid."

He nodded. "Oh, yeah. We rarely stayed in one place for more than a few months at a time."

"Wow, that had to be rough, changing schools all the time."

"I never went to school."

Her eyes went wide at that. "But you're a college professor."

He laughed. "Assistant professor," he corrected her. "It'll be a while before I can apply to be a full professor. But I'm working on it."

She made an impatient face, then said, "But you're an assistant college professor. How could you have never attended school?"

"Some people might call me homeschooled. More like I'm a graduate of the school of life."

"I'm not sure I understand."

He sighed. The moon had risen more since they had sat down, and the sky was fast growing dark. A few dozen stars had made an appearance in the night sky, twinkling like tiny gems. Pax thought again about the drive back to Ithaca tonight and how he should have been on the road an hour ago. Then he realized he didn't care. He didn't have to teach tomorrow, and he'd driven later than this plenty of times. And he was with Emma. Talking about things that would help them get to know each other better. In that moment, there was nothing he wanted more. Worst-case scenario, they stayed out here on the dock all night talking and he mainlined a couple quarts of coffee in the morning before he drove home. Then again, sitting out here all night talking to Emma was the best-case scenario, too.

"Pretty much everything I knew before I went to college," he said, "I learned on my own. My grandmother—

though she probably wasn't really my grandmother any more than my cousins and aunts and uncles were really my cousins and aunts and uncles—taught me to read. After that, there was no stopping me from learning whatever I wanted to know."

"Okay, I'm really lost now," she told him. "You just said you come from a big family, and now you're saying all those people probably weren't really family."

"Where I come from, the term *family* means something completely different from what most people think. It doesn't mean you necessarily have blood ties to another person. It means you live the same way they do and share the same experiences as them." He decided he might as well tell her what else had defined his family. "And also that you all watch out for each other and lie if the authorities come looking for one of you."

She studied him hard. "Should I be concerned? Because that kind of sounds more like the Manson Family."

He couldn't help smiling sadly at that. "Not exactly. Though I will be honest with you and confess that crime really was the way we made our living. Just not violent crime."

Her concern seemed to grow with every word he said. "I remember you telling me that first day we met that your parents, um, weren't exactly truthful all the time."

Wow, he had told her that right off the bat, hadn't he? How weird. Not that he made any big secret about his upbringing, but he usually didn't, well, bring it up that early in a relationship. Not that he and Emma even had a relationship, not really—not yet—but for him to have told her that within minutes of meeting her just went to show how comfortable he'd been with her the second they met.

She continued, "Now you're saying your family wasn't exactly, or at least maybe not biologically, your family."

"Yeah, it's complicated," Pax said with much understatement.

"Sounds like."

"Some of us were for sure blood relatives, but some of us were just folks who wandered in." He sighed again. "My parents—the people who mostly raised me—were liars." There was no way, or reason, to sugarcoat that. "The rest of my family were liars, too." He met her gaze levelly when he added, "I was also a liar when I was young. Until I learned better. Like I said, that's how we made our living. Lying. Conning. Stealing. And as soon as we kids were old enough to take part in those cons, we were enlisted to lie, con and steal, too."

Her mouth actually dropped open a little in surprise at that.

"I grew up in a band of vagabonds and renegades," he told her point-blank. "There. That makes me sound romantic and glamorous, doesn't it? Completely skirts the fact that we were professional criminals who traveled all over the country stealing from whoever we could."

She studied him in silence for a moment, as if she didn't believe him. Him, the man who never, under any circumstances, told a lie.

Finally she said, "I'm sorry, but that sounds like something from a movie. And I'm having a lot of trouble seeing you in an environment like that. You're such a decent guy."

No greater compliment had ever been paid Pax than being called *decent*. He didn't care if other people considered the word a thinly veiled disparagement or a meaningless platitude. Considering the people he'd grown up around, being called decent was a badge of honor.

"Thanks," he told her. "I like to think that I am. Now. But that wasn't always the case. I learned at an early age how to manipulate and use people. It's how I was raised."

"This sounds like an interesting story," she said, "but it also sounds like one you might not want to share. So if you don't…"

She left the statement open ended, but her meaning was clear: she didn't want to pry into his life any more than he did hers. But she obviously still wanted to know more about him, the same way he wanted to know more about her. He could tell her that, like Dickinson College, this was a story for another time. But she had shared her less-than-idyllic past with him tonight and been honest about it. And he was surprised to discover he really did want to share his with her. Knowing she cane from origins that hadn't been much happier than his own made him feel as if they were two of a kind.

"Nah, it's fine," he said. "I'm just not sure where to begin."

"A lot of people think the best place to begin is the beginning."

Okay, then. He would start at the beginning, as well as he could remember it. "Lightfoot is the last name on my birth certificate, but I don't know if that was the real name of my birth parents or just something they made up that sounded good. All of us had forged documents for IDs. I have a Social Security number, but I'm reasonably certain it belonged to someone else before it belonged to me. At the time I was born, the internet was still in its infancy, so it was a lot easier to fudge that stuff."

She nodded at that. "Yeah, these days you can't just pop into the Office of Vital Statistics and submit a request in paper with a fake ID and walk off free and clear. There's always going to be some kind of trace thanks to all the protocols that have been put in place to battle phishing and smishing and vishing."

Now Pax was the one to be confused. How did she know about all that stuff?

"I mean, that's what I've read," she said when she saw his expression. "You can't be too careful these days. So how did your family work its scams?"

"Sometimes it was as blatant as just driving through the wealthy neighborhoods in a city and finding someone who was out gardening or watering their lawn. Then one person would provide a distraction while another went through the back door and ransacked the place." He hesitated before adding, "There were a lot of times when I was the distraction. We kids would ride a bike past the house and fake an accident so the person outside—often an elderly person," he added with the all-too-familiar bad taste in his mouth, "would come into the street to help us. If we could manage to make ourselves bleed, all the better. That meant more time for our partner to grab whatever they could."

Emma gazed at him in clear distress. "That's awful, that they used children for something like that."

"Smart, too," he said with both admiration and disgust. "A lot of people will walk away from an adult in trouble. But a kid? There aren't many who won't come to their aid. And that innate kindness in those people is what my family took advantage of."

Pax could still scarcely believe the details of his own childhood, even having lived them. It really was unconscionable, what he and his "family" had done when he was a kid. What the rest of them were still out there doing, as far as he knew. As good as they'd all been at stealing and conning, they were even better at evading the law.

"When I and some of the other kids got old enough to use a computer, the grown-ups steered us toward cyber-crimes. That's mostly what I was doing when I left. All the -*ishings* weren't really a thing yet at that point, but I was excellent at hacking. I could get into just about any bank account anywhere and drain it dry. I wanted to go after corporations—especially the ones that were polluting the planet or using slave labor overseas—because we could have made a ton of money in one fell swoop. But the elders said no, that big businesses have huge legal teams and enough money to put the heat on finding and burying the culprit, so we had to focus on the poor and disenfranchised instead. People who couldn't afford attorneys to help them get their money back or who didn't trust the cops enough to even report the thefts."

He expelled a sound of self-loathing. "I still can't believe I did that to people. I wish I could go back in time and return everything I ever stole from anyone."

A few inches separated him and Emma on the dock, and both were leaning back with their hands against the wood. She straightened, moving her hand to cover his. "You were a kid," she said softly. "One who was raised by people who taught you badly."

"I was old enough to know by then that what I was doing was wrong," he corrected her.

"You were still a kid," she insisted. "And kids do what they're told by the people who have authority over them when they don't think they have any other alternatives." Her hand on his tightened. "And you did obviously turn your back on that life eventually."

He nodded. "I was sixteen when I started to realize just how awful my family was and how wrong what they were doing was."

"What happened?"

"A con for my folks that ultimately went bad. For them, at least. Before the beard came in, I could always pass for a lot younger than I was. Long story short, my parents were running a con on this elderly lady when they found out she had recently lost her son and daughter-in-law and grandson in a car accident. When she showed them a photo of the family, they realized her thirteen-year-old grandson looked almost exactly like me and that his father, her son, probably looked like both of us when he was a kid. They had me cozy up to her, knowing she would have a soft spot for a kid who looked like the grandson and son she'd lost less than a year ago. They figured keeping her grief alive every day like that would make the con go a lot faster and they'd be able to milk her of a lot more money."

As he always did when he thought about Mrs. Aebersold, Pax got a little nauseous. She'd been a nice lady. From the minute he met her, she had felt like a grandmother to him. But not the kind who traveled with his family, who only tolerated the kids long enough to teach them a new con or relieve them of the money they made that day. Mrs. Aebersold had been the kind he'd read about in books, who baked pies and played board games and sewed patches on ripped jeans. Which were all things she did for and with him at one time or another.

She also played her favorite music for him, golden-age jazz and old standards, and she introduced him to her favorite movies and books—she'd really loved Sam Spade, and to this day, *Casablanca* was Pax's favorite film. The more time he'd spent with her, the better he'd gotten to know her. And the better he'd gotten to know her, the less he'd wanted to steal anything from her. On the contrary, one day he realized he would do whatever he could to protect her from people like his parents.

That was the day he told her who he really was and why he had come into her life. He returned every cent of the money his parents—and he—had taken from her, and he told her what to do to make sure she protected herself from people like them in the future. And he apologized. Profusely. Then he walked away. From her and his family and a way of life he finally realized was toxic, destructive, and evil.

In one final act of fraud, he forged all the documents he would need to move on with his life—a fake high school transcript with an exceptionally good GPA, letters of recommendation from doting—and nonexistent— teachers, rosters of phony volunteering and community service gigs, tax forms for bogus parents that would provide him with proof for need-based financial aid. He'd relied on the hope that admissions personnel at the colleges to which he applied were either too overworked or too careless to check all the documents he sent. Doubtless, there had been some who figured they were being scammed and either rejected his application or ignored it. But he had been accepted to a few places, one of which he enrolled in.

With an actual college degree—and being as good at computers as he was—it had been a lot easier to be accepted into a master's program. And with the connections he made earning his master's, moving on to the PhD program had been even easier. No one at Cornell had a clue that Pax wasn't everything he'd made himself to be when he was seventeen. To them, he was a respected member of the faculty and a shining example of just how successful their students could be. Even if he'd begun his academic career fraudulently, he'd earned every degree and accolade legitimately. He hadn't lied once since the day he made himself a high school superstar with no financial means of support. And he would never lie again.

By the time he finished telling all this to Emma, night had well and truly fallen, and it was past his usual bedtime. He didn't care. It had felt good telling her everything. He'd carried that onus alone for more than a decade. No one he knew now had a clue about the truth of his past. Emma was the first person he'd told. And sharing it all with her made him feel as if a massive weight had fallen from his back.

The crickets had all gone to sleep by now, so the air around them was silent, save for the lapping of the water against the dock. In the pale moonlight, he could see that Emma had hung on every word and now looked at him as if she were processing everything he'd said.

"Do you know where Mrs. Aebersold is now?" It was the last question he would have expected after all he'd told her.

He nodded. "She's still around. She has a Facebook and Insta account. Both public. I'm not sure she knows how to make them private. I check in on both from time to time."

"How is she doing?"

"Good, as far as I can tell," he said. "She remarried a few years ago to a guy who has children and grandchildren. She shares pics of them a lot and calls them her grandkids, too. She seems happy."

"Do you ever think about contacting her?"

"Think about it, yes," he admitted. "But I'd never do it."

"Why not?"

"I can't think of a single reason why I should hurt that poor woman all over again."

"She might like to talk to you."

"I sincerely doubt that."

"People can be surprising."

He knew that. He did. And it was possible Mrs. Aebersold might forgive him for his part in what had happened. But Pax wasn't about to revisit that sorry chapter of his life again. Not even to make reparations. Because, honestly, he didn't think there were reparations enough in the world to undo all the harm he and his family had done.

"I'm just glad that part of my life is over," he said. "Even though there's a part of me that will never be entirely free of it."

She nodded as if she understood. "I have to believe something good will always come out of a bad time. Whether it's a lesson learned or new philosophy forged or a friend made or…" She smiled. "Whatever. There just must be something good somewhere in a rough patch to make it mean something and give it a reason for happening in the first place."

Once again, she seemed to be talking about something specific, but Pax couldn't imagine what it was. Probably, her first few years away from home hadn't been the best. But she'd landed in a good place now, as far as he could see. Who wouldn't feel better sitting in a place like this on such a beautiful night?

"Thanks," he said. "I hope you're right."

"I am," she said confidently. "A year ago, I might not have believed that, but I do now."

Well, that was a cryptic statement just begging for clarity. But like so much else they'd talked about tonight, it was for another time. Because if some things between him and Emma remained unclear, there was one thing that was crystal: There would be another time. And another after that. Hopefully there would be an infinite number of other times for them in the future. But for now, he'd just look forward to the next one.

He glanced down at his watch. It was even later than he'd thought. "Wow. I really need to be going. I'm sorry I kept you up so late yammering at you."

"I'm not sorry at all," she said. Softly and tentatively, to be sure, but she'd put it out there just the same, and without a single hesitation.

The wind kicked up off the water, nudging her bangs into her eyes. Without thinking about what he was doing, Pax reached up to move her hair back at the same time she did so herself. Their hands connected at her temple, and they both stopped, fingers twined, gazes fixed. Time seemed to stop in that moment. The silence of the night was as deep as its darkness, and the splash of the water and the ripple of the wind died to a whisper. Not sure why he did it, simply feeling like it was the perfect moment for it, he dipped his head toward hers. Emma leaned in, too, as if she were caught in the same spell as he. Closer and closer they came together, until a scant inch separated their mouths.

Then, out of nowhere, a loon called out, a long, soft, haunting call followed by a trio of quiet hoots. Emma turned her head toward the lake at the sound, and the moment—the kiss—was gone. The loon's cry was immediately answered by another, this one an even longer, eerier lament. Within seconds, other loons joined in, until one cry after another turned into a chorus of unearthly music.

"This is amazing," she whispered with both reverence and delight. "I've never heard loons do that. I'd never heard a loon at all before I came here, and even then, it's only been an occasional one at night. I didn't know they could sound like this. It's..."

She stopped when she couldn't conjure a word that would do justice to what they were hearing. Normally Pax would have agreed and been as enraptured as she was. But he'd heard loons lots of times in his travels. And these had just cost him a kiss he'd very much wanted to enjoy.

Another time, he told himself. Another time *soon*.

"They're gorgeous birds," he agreed. "I'm surprised you never heard one before coming here, though. They're all over the place."

"I've never really lived outside of cities and towns before now," she said. She looked around—at the lake, the stars, the moon, all of it. "This place isn't like anyplace I've ever been. I'm not sure I'll ever want to leave here."

Pax hoped she never left here, either. Unless it was to move closer to him.

With much reluctance, he stood, giving his surroundings one last look himself. He really had lived everywhere, even in places like this. But Emma was right. There was something about Sudbury that made it feel different somehow.

He extended a hand and helped her up, then waited while she slipped her sandals back on. As they made their way up the deck, back toward the mansion, they reached for each other's hands and wove their fingers together, as if it were the most natural thing in the world for them to do. Whatever was happening between him and Emma felt like the natural conclusion to a long series of events neither had planned or wanted. As if this was their reward for surviving times and things that hadn't been so great when they happened. Pax felt better in this moment than he'd felt in a very long time. Maybe forever. And somewhere deep inside himself, he somehow knew it was only going to get better.

"You sure you'll be okay to drive back to Ithaca?" she asked as they came to a stop by his car. "I'm sure Haven and Bennett could find a room for you to spend the night in if you want."

"Nah, I'll be okay," he assured her. "It'll be like the old days, when I was doing my undergrad, driving back to campus in the middle of the night from a concert. Except it's not the middle of the night—yet—and those drives were a lot longer than an hour."

"Text me when you get home so I know you made it okay."

Pax smiled. He couldn't remember the last time anyone had asked him to do that. Probably, an old girlfriend had at some point. But he didn't remember who.

One minor thing, though. "Gonna be hard to do that when I don't have your number," he told her.

She held out her hand for his phone. He dutifully pulled it from his pocket, punched in his code and gave it to her. She found his contacts and typed in her number, along with her name. Which she must have messed up, because she ended up typing a lot more than four letters. When he took the phone back, he halfway expected to see some cutesy nickname she'd given herself. But all it said was *Emma B*. As if he knew so many Emmas, she'd had to put her last initial in there. He stuck the phone back into one pocket as he withdrew his keys from the other.

"Good night, Emma B," he told her.

"Good night, Pax," she replied with a small smile.

Before he realized what she was going to do, she lifted a hand and cupped it over his jaw, stroking his beard idly with her fingers. He felt that touch all the way to his soul and lifted his own hand to cover hers. For one long moment, they only gazed into each other's eyes, as if neither knew what to say to the other but didn't want to part ways. He was about to bend to kiss her again, but those damned loons started up again. They laughed lightly, then Emma pushed herself up onto her toes to brush a kiss on the cheek she wasn't holding, her soft mouth skimming the skin on the ridge of his jaw. It happened so quickly, he almost thought he imagined it. Except for the warm sensation that lingered where she had touched him. And okay, in a few other places, too.

"Thank you for a nice evening," she said breathlessly as she lowered herself again and dropped her hand back to her side.

"Thank you for a nice evening, too," he replied.

"Guess I'll see you when I see you."

He nodded, climbed into his car and started the engine. Then he gave her one last longing look before throwing the car into Drive and lifting a hand out the open window as he drove off. He couldn't think of a single reason why he would need to come back to Summerlight in the foreseeable future. But he would, without question, be coming back to Summerlight in the foreseeable future.

Just as soon as he could figure out a plausible excuse that didn't make it sound like he was lying.

Chapter Six

She hadn't said a single thing tonight that wasn't true.

As Emma lay awake in her bed long after Pax finally headed back to Ithaca, she marveled at how honest she had been able to be the entire time they talked—both at dinner and, later, on the dock. Okay, maybe some of what she'd told him had only been true because of evasion and creative punctuation, but all of it *had* been true. She *had* traveled across the country at one point, and she *had* spent time on the West Coast. Yes, she'd grown up on the other side of the country and not Pennsylvania, and yes, crossing from the West Coast to the East had happened over the past year, not a decade ago. Both statements had still been true. And she had seen all those sights she told him about after leaving home. She just hadn't had to drive as far as he assumed to do it at that point, since she'd grown up in Idaho. At the time, she'd been experimenting with where she wanted to live and what she wanted to do, and she'd moved around a lot and worked a number of jobs for the first three or four years after leaving home. She'd ultimately settled in Seattle, thanks to the plethora of tech jobs there, and she'd liked the city a lot. Enough to stay there forever, had her life not been upended the way it had.

Even the facts she'd spoken about Altoona—although she might have been saying them from memorization to further convince Pax she was Emma Brown, not Amber Finch—had all been true. And her opinions, thoughts and observations during dinner with him and Haven and Bennett? Also true. All had come from *her* heart and *her* brain. She had no idea if the real Emma Brown was a fan of the Marvel Universe, and she might very well have hated chicken caprese. The Emma Brown formerly known as Amber Finch hadn't had any trouble at all espousing her sincere thoughts and opinions and likes and dislikes.

Okay, so she'd dodged a bullet by telling him that her experience at Dickinson College was a story for another time. That, too, had been true. She would tell him about Dickinson—and how she'd never been a student there or a housekeeper at a hotel in the same town— eventually. She'd tell him the truth about everything eventually. As soon as she knew him well enough to be certain she could trust him.

All that said, though, she doubted Pax would appreciate the nuances of her subterfuge once he did discover the truth. He'd been pretty adamant about how he didn't think there was a single good reason for lying and how he couldn't forgive deception under any circumstances. She guessed if she'd grown up the way he had, she might feel the same way about the world. But the world wasn't black and white. Not everything was a matter of true or false. There was always wiggle room with just about everything, and there were some situations where not being quite honest was perfectly okay. It wasn't healthy to see everything—or anything—in terms of absolutes. But she supposed that if a person hadn't grown up with a healthy outlook, it was easy to fall into thinking that it was.

Tonight, though, she had been absolute, and she hadn't spoken one lie. Not one. For the first time in nearly a year, she'd had a conversation with someone that hadn't had any fabrications in it at all. A conversation so heartfelt and so enjoyable that she'd honestly forgotten at times in the evening that she was supposed to be careful with whatever she said. But even forgetting that, she hadn't lied. Not once. Pax had just put her so at ease that, for the first time in almost a year, she'd been able to be her true self. It was just too bad she'd done nothing but lie to him prior to this evening.

No, that's not true, she immediately reassured herself. That day they'd shared lunch in Sudbury, she had been honest about everything then, too. When she'd spoken of Emma Brown that day, she'd spoken of her in the third person, not the first, and what she'd said about Emma was true. True, too, had been the part about how Pax was a very good—very decent—guy.

But—and it was a big *but*—he was still a member of a community, even if from the fringes, that wanted to do her harm. She'd learned almost as soon as entering the World Wide Web as a teenager that the internet could be a scary place, with lots of scary people. That had only been hammered home over the past nine months. No, knowing what she did of Pax so far, he wasn't one of those miscreants who wanted to come after her for the simple crime of being a woman with an opinion. She sincerely doubted he'd ever given more than a passing thought to Travis Swope, if that. She hadn't seen anything so far to suggest there was anything toxic about his masculinity. But there was still that matter of a huge pile of money waiting for anyone who turned her in. Although Pax didn't seem like the kind of guy to be driven by money, either—especially after what he'd told her tonight about his former family—she still couldn't be too careful. Not yet.

But she *would* tell him the truth about everything, once she knew him better and knew without doubt that she could trust him. In the meantime, she would just do everything she could to be honest with him. As long as they stayed off of specifics, that shouldn't be too difficult. As long as they talked about themselves personally, their dreams and life philosophies, their opinions about the day-to-day workings of existing on this planet, they would be fine.

She thought again about their near kiss on the dock. She had no idea what had come over her to almost let that happen. There had just been something in that moment that had been so… She expelled a restless sound. She didn't even know what had made that moment different from a million others. Except that Pax had been at the center of it, looking handsome and thoughtful and vulnerable, a combination that made him sexy as hell. The moonlight had washed over him in a way that made him look almost otherworldly. In that moment, he kind of had been. Emma's experiences with men weren't vast, but she'd certainly had more than a couple of relationships and even more boyfriends. But she'd never met a man like Pax, so sweet and inviting one minute and so hot and arousing the next.

Something warm and pleasant blossomed in her mid-section and began to seep outward, flowing into every part of her body, easing all the knots of tension and ter-ror that had been her companions for too long. Mus-cles she hadn't even been aware of clenching started to loosen, and thoughts she hadn't realized were dark began to draw light. The stress that had weighed on her for so many months began to ease, and in some weary part of her brain, she began to remember what life could be like without the choking specter of doom following her every step. Happiness. That was what she was starting to feel again. It had been so long, she almost didn't recognize it.

Whatever was happening between her and Pax—though she was pretty sure she knew what was hap-pening between her and Pax—she didn't want to do anything to mess it up. Yeah, okay, she'd come into the situation already messing it up by having to pre-tend to be someone she wasn't. She had a good rea-son for that. Her very survival. Pax would eventually come to understand once she explained everything to him. He'd done what he had to do to survive, too, once upon a time. He'd lived through a period where he was dishonest himself before turning his back on the only life he'd ever known. In a way, he'd become someone he wasn't, too. But it was a better version of himself.

Or maybe he'd just become the person he was always supposed to be. Emma had changed a lot, too, since she'd fled Seattle. Gone was the loudmouth, filter-free, speak-her-mind-and-all-else-be-damned hellion she grew into after leaving home. She'd been a quiet, diffident child when she lived with her parents. Once she was out from under their thumb, the pendulum had swung completely to the other side, and she'd been as in-your-face about everything as she possibly could be. She'd told herself at the time she was just being honest and saying what everyone else was thinking anyway. Now, though, she realized she had just been pushing boundaries and crossing lines to see what she could get away with.

Okay, okay. She'd been an obnoxious jerk.

Now, though, she knew better. Boundary-pushing and line-crossing could be healthy to a point. Beyond that point, it could be, at best, insufferable and, at worst, dangerous. Emma had lived as two extremes in her life so far—compliant child and annoying adult. Neither incarnation of her had been happy, not really. Neither had been healthy. Neither had been her. The last almost year had brought a lot of adjustments in her actions and thoughts and observations. Those adjustments had altered her personality, too. She was still learning who she actually was. Who she honestly was. Maybe the more time she spent with Pax, the better she would get to know herself. Her true self. Maybe she could become the person she was always supposed to be, too.

She turned onto her side and looked out the window. Clouds had moved in, and the moon had ducked behind one. Only a handful of stars defied them, twinkling through the few openings they could find. Emma smiled at the sight. She kind of felt like one of those stars at the moment—finding the cracks in the clouds to shine through them as brightly as they could.

She would get there. Maybe not tomorrow. Maybe not next week. It might take months or even years before she finally found her real self. But that was okay. She was safe here in Sudbury. She was calm here. She was happy here. Best of all, Pax was here with her, to help her play the breaks.

With any luck, they would both be able to stay here once they learned the truth about who Emma Brown— and Amber Finch—really were.

It was another week before Pax could make his way back to Summerlight. Not because he needed time to manufacture a reason—he figured wanting to see Emma was all the reason he needed now—but because life kept getting in the way. First, he'd had to sub again for a couple of days for an instructor who had a family emergency, then he'd had to finish putting together the syllabi for his fall courses so they could be approved. Then he'd had to start on another article for another journal since that *publish-or-perish* thing he'd always thought was hyperbole in the novels he'd read and movies he'd seen as a kid was actually not hyperbole at all.

But he did finally get back to Summerlight the weekend following the one when he had dinner with Emma and Haven and Bennett. There had been a time in Pax's life when he would have thought having to drive an hour to see someone would have prevented him from seeing that person ever again. Who was worth that much trouble? But driving an hour to see Emma seemed like no time at all. And even if it had, she was more than worth the trouble. There was no trouble when it came to Emma. He didn't think he'd ever been able to say that about anyone. So what was a quick jaunt north to spend a little time with her?

He'd even spruced up for the trip, donning his favorite shirt—this one white, spattered with colorful mid-century-modern starbursts—and halfway decent pants. Yeah, okay, they were denim in nature, but they were still a damned sight nicer than the baggy cargos he usually wore this time of year.

Haven was in the foyer when Pax strode through Summerlight's front door, her tool belt riding low on her hips, which meant she was in the middle of some major project that required a lot of mechanics. She took one look at him, grinned and said, "She's upstairs in the ballroom, cleaning. But I'm sure she'll be breaking for lunch in—" She grabbed her phone from one of the tool belt's many pockets to see the time. "Ten… nine…eight…" She looked at Pax again. "Why are you still standing here? You're going to totally mess up my prediction."

She didn't have to tell him twice. He spun on his heel and made his way toward the sweeping main staircase, taking the steps two at a time. The ballroom was at the top of the stairs, the centerpiece of the second floor, whose east and west wings extended down each side. There was a time when it had actually been a ballroom, hosting scores, maybe even hundreds, of guests, who'd partied like it was 1899. Haven planned on using it now as a meeting and reception hall, primarily for weddings but also for businesses that might need such a space. That last idea hadn't inspired her to make the cavernous room more businesslike, however. She'd definitely considered the wedding angle primarily and returned the room to its original, overly ornate self.

She'd discovered from her lots-of-greats-grandmother's journal—she and her husband had been the mansion's original owners—that, originally, the ballroom's hardwood floor had gleamed like honey and the walls had been pearly white, their wainscoting trimmed in gold. So Haven had recreated it that way down to the last square inch. The ceiling, though, had been a bit tougher for her to refurbish on her own, and since it was the room's—maybe even the whole house's—centerpiece, she'd been adamant that the ceiling, too, be brought back to its original life. In Summerlight's heyday, it had been painted with a sweeping mural by a famous Finger Lakes region artist, who had depicted a romanticized image of the sky for each season. By the time Haven and Bennett inherited the place, that painting had been soiled and faded and neglected to the point of becoming nearly indistinct. Pax had seen it in that condition, and it had been crushing to realize something that had once been so beautiful had become so decayed.

But Bennett had found an art conservator-restorer through the Metropolitan Museum of Art in New York City, who had come in after Christmas and gone right to work. The project was almost finished, Pax saw when he entered the ballroom now, and he was amazed at the difference. The center of the ceiling was a pale, well, sky blue, which gradually darkened to midnight where the ceiling met the walls. In between were all manner of heavenly bodies, from planets, stars, comets and nebulae to cherubs, seraphim and sky gods and goddesses from more ancient cultures than even he, voracious, life-long library patron that he was, could identify.

And in the far corner, under an image of what appeared to be... *Eos and Nyx maybe?* he wondered, even though, admittedly, he only knew those deities from video games, which the original artist never would have seen. Anyway, under images of two otherworldly mythical immortals of the sky was Pax's own, very real, goddess—this one of Truth and Beauty—Emma Brown.

He knew he should stop thinking of her as a goddess of anything, let alone truth and beauty. She'd gone out of her way to assure him she was just plain ol' Emma Brown from Altoona, Pennsylvania, and she seemed like the kind of woman who would probably smack anyone who called her a goddess. If she'd wanted to present herself as a goddess, she never would have copped to always being an also-ran—someone who won a red ribbon at the county fair when she could have said she won a blue one at state level, and who barely made it into the homecoming court when she could have said she was homecoming queen. And she certainly never would have told him she'd grown up in a trailer park and barely finished high school when she could have said her family was one of Altoona's finest and that she'd graduated at the top of her class in one of those tony country day schools.

Hell, who needed a goddess, something mythical and untrue, when you could find the real thing? Which was exactly what Emma was—genuine, down-to-earth, honest. Finding someone like her was way better than encountering a goddess.

She was wearing a different skirt today—good to know she did have one or two other wardrobe options—this one printed with some kind of batik pattern and paired with a black T-shirt. She was on her hands and knees in the corner of the room, wiping along the base-boards, humming a song Pax kind of recognized, but maybe not. He wondered why she didn't have in ear-buds, listening to her phone. It occurred to him then that he'd never actually seen her with a phone, something he found curious now. He always had his phone on him, tucked into a pocket. It was practically an ex-tension of his body, one of those never-leave-home-without-it things. But she must have a phone, because she'd punched her number into his the other night, and he'd texted her when he got back to Ithaca, the way she'd made him promise to do. More to the point, she'd texted him back. Maybe it was just one of those women-don't-get-pockets wardrobe problems he'd read about online.

He was about to announce his presence from the en-tryway when she suddenly screamed, jumped up and started dancing around as if she were on hot lava. She grabbed the back of her neck with one hand and the hem of her shirt with the other, wagging it back and forth as she then sent the other hand knifing through her hair, brushing something invisible off her shoulders, and just generally whirled around like the Tasmanian Devil in an old cartoon. And she never stopped squealing. Pax shouted her name in panic and ran across the room to help with whatever was wrong.

When she saw him, she stopped squealing incoherently long enough to say, "Spider! Giant spider! It dropped onto my neck, and I think it went down my shirt. Or into my hair or…or…or… *Spider!*" she then shouted even more loudly. *"Giant spider! Help!"*

Pax did his best, but the way she kept dancing around made it a little difficult. Finally, he grabbed her gently by both arms and made her stand still so he could see if there was anything giant and arachnid in nature crawling on her anywhere.

"Get it, get it, get it," she whispered in clear panic.

"I don't see it," he told her.

"It's on me. I know it. I can feel it."

"Where?"

"Everywhere."

Well, that was super helpful.

He gave her another quick once-over. Nothing on her front. So he spun her still-trembling body around until her back was to him. Nothing on her back, either. But she was still muttering *Get it get it get it!* with much distress. So he took the hem of her shirt gingerly between two fingers and shook it. But nothing fell out. She was still shaking, though, and now making a noise like an injured animal. So he patted the shirt against her back to double check. No spider. No bra, either, he couldn't help noticing, since he was only human, but no spider. Just to be triply sure, he moved his hand to the neck of her shirt and started to pull it toward him, just to take a quick peek down her back to be certain there truly was nothing there, and—

And might as well have just turned into a giant spider himself. Because Emma suddenly jerked away from him, spinning around with enough force to nearly topple herself. She only kept herself from a tornadic disaster by planting a hand firmly against the wall beside her. Her fear of being invaded by a spider suddenly evaporated, to be replaced by what he could only identify as revulsion toward him. Okay, he'd been about to look down her shirt. But only the back of it, and only because she was telling him to *Get it get it get it!* with all the urgency of an ambulance driver who had a woman in labor in the back. There hadn't been anything untoward or threatening in his gesture. But she was looking at him as if he'd been about to strip her naked and burn her at the stake.

"What?" he said. "I just wanted to make sure there was nothing down your shirt."

But her hand was fastened to her nape with the back of her shirt pressed hard between them. And she was glaring at him as if he'd tried to pour a whole jar of spiders down her shirt himself.

"There's nothing down my shirt," she told him coldly.

"You seemed to think there was a couple of seconds ago."

"There is nothing down my shirt," she repeated even more icily. "Never do that again."

"Okay," he said, still wondering why she was so mad. She'd been terrified. What else was he supposed to do? He held up both hands in front of himself in a gesture of surrender and told her, "I'm sorry. You asked me for help. I was just trying to help you."

She continued to study him menacingly for another minute, then, little by little, she began to relax. She released her shirt and shook it out, then did the same for her skirt. Then, her gaze still fixed with his—and still filled with wariness—she scrubbed both hands through her hair. Whatever she'd felt had descended upon her from above was evidently gone now. Not gone was her very clear distrust of Pax.

"Are you okay?" he asked.

She nodded slowly. Warily. "I just don't like spiders."

"Yeah, I could kinda tell."

She tugged her shirt down a bit, brushed a hand over her skirt, ran her fingers through her hair one more time, and tugged her shirt down again. She inhaled a deep breath and released it slowly.

"No, I'm sorry," she told him. "I overreacted. I know you were only trying to help."

He nodded. But he was no more okay with what had just happened than Emma was. Her response to his effort to render aid had gone beyond an overreaction. It had been out-and-out terror. Which, sure, he could understand in relation to the spider. He didn't have a problem with them, but he could understand why some people did. But Emma had no reason to be that frightened— that terrified—of him.

Pax understood well the concept of consent when it

came to the whole man-woman thing. Probably better than most people, since he spent so much time browsing social media online and read complaints from women, especially, about men who went too far without permission or thought. He was generally pretty cautious when it came to interactions with women, both because he didn't want to be rude, and he didn't want to come across as menacing. But when someone shouted about giant spiders and specifically asked for help, deliberation kinda went out the window and action took over.

He didn't want to think about *why* Emma might have overreacted the way she did. Because it had been the kind of response that came when a person's agency over their own body had been violated in some way. He remembered, too, how wary she'd been of him that first day they met and how she'd deliberately kept a good physical distance between them. The thought that someone might have done something to her that caused her to be so mistrustful hit him in a place where he'd only been hit once before: When he finally realized just how badly his family was treating Mrs. Aebersold. And how he had been a part of that treatment until he came to his senses. He didn't want to divide the world into two categories, predator and prey, but after some of the things he'd seen and read about—and done—it was hard not to.

"Are you okay?" he asked Emma now. It was the kind of open-ended question that, depending on her reply, offered the opportunity for her to either speak at length and share any abuse she may have suffered or to just drop the subject.

"I'm fine," she said.

Okay, then. Subject dropped. But not forgotten.

There was a moment of awkward silence, as if she were waiting for him to press for more details. When he didn't, she asked, point-blank, "What are you doing here?"

He told himself not to take the question the wrong way, and truly, the way she'd said it hadn't sounded like she didn't want him there. But he supposed it could be considered odd that he'd just show up out of nowhere the way he had. He'd originally planned on telling her that he came up here exclusively to see her. Considering what had just happened, though, he was thinking now that maybe telling her that would just put her on the spot. So he used his backup reason instead.

Okay, okay. Maybe there was a part of him that hadn't been all that confident that Emma would welcome his arrival as much as he'd hoped she would. And hey, had it not been for the spider incident, she might very well have. It was possible.

Anyway.

"I came up to film some video of Summerlight," he told her.

Her brows knit down again in that way he was coming to realize meant she didn't like what she was hearing or what was going on *at all*. But all she said was "Video?"

He nodded. "For some promo for the inn."

"What kind of promo for the inn?" she asked.

He remembered then that Emma hadn't come out onto the patio last weekend until after he and Haven had bounced around their idea, so she hadn't heard the exchange.

"I've been putting up bits of video about the inn on its website and social media for a while now. Just little two- or three-minute snippets to show the donors from the crowdfunding how their money is being spent and to create more interest for the place."

Her brows knit down even farther. "Have you done any of that lately?" she asked.

It wasn't exactly the way he'd expected her to take interest, but he replied, "Not for a few weeks."

"How many weeks?"

Again, an odd response. "I don't know. Maybe a month?"

"Have you done it since I've been here?"

He shook his head. And wondered why she would ask. "No. I haven't really been up here that much since before—" He was about to confess he'd barely been around before she showed up but stopped himself. Instead he said, "It was tough making the time for it during the spring semester."

She nodded slowly, and her expression cleared. Some. "So what are you going to be filming today?"

"Whatever looks interesting," he told her. "Haven suggested I do something more in-depth than just teaser reels about the place. Kind of a before and after of the whole house's rehab that could potentially be long enough to qualify for a short-feature-type thing. It could appeal to all the DIY geeks out there and maybe gain some traction and be shared a lot. Become kind of an advertisement for the place without looking like an advertisement for the place."

Her expression finally cleared at the explanation. "Oh. That actually sounds like a really good idea."

"Right?" Pax agreed. "She said she's been taking video since she and Bennett first moved in. She's got some great footage showing what a sad state the mansion was in when they first arrived and some progress footage of different projects that were the most challenging."

Emma looked up at the ballroom ceiling, then back at Pax. "She showed me photos of how bad it was here in the ballroom before Bennett had the restorers come in for the ceiling. It's amazing what they accomplished just with that. I can see where someone could produce a whole documentary about this place for Netflix or something."

"Oh, that's an even better idea," he said, wondering why he hadn't thought of that himself. Haven probably had hundreds of hours of video she'd taken over the past eight or nine months. "Anyway, I thought I probably should start taking advantage of my time off whenever I could since classes are going to be starting up at Cornell again in about a month and a half. Time flies, and all that. Plus, it would be good to capture the inn at different times of the year since Haven is hoping to keep the place full regardless of the season. She and Bennett weren't here last summer, so…" He shrugged. "I'm probably going to be up here pretty regularly between now and the end of August."

There. Now he had an excuse to come to Summerlight whenever he wanted to. And it was a totally legit one.

At this, Emma's expression clouded again for some

reason. "You're going to be filming all summer?" she asked.

Why did she seem so worried about that? "Early fall, too," he said. "Haven and Bennett didn't move in until late October last year. Even without the longer feature, I'm planning on posting short snippets here and there about seasonal changes and preparations that are only a couple minutes long. Mood pieces mostly. It's why I came up this afternoon. The weather's really nice today, and I want to capture the inn at golden hour."

"Golden hour?"

He nodded. "I want to catch some images of the place in the long, slanting late-afternoon sunlight. And maybe some twilight footage, too. After the other night, when you and I were out on the dock, it occurred to me just how beautiful this place really is and how that beauty differs at various points in the day."

His mention of the weekend before had the desired effect. Two bright spots of pink bloomed on Emma's cheeks, and her lips curled into a soft smile. "That was a nice night," she said softly.

He smiled back. "Yeah, it was." He wanted to add that they should do it again soon. Like, maybe…oh, he didn't know…tonight.

But before he could, she returned to the matter of the video. "You and Haven are smart. That should be some nice promo for the place."

Fine. They'd keep talking about that instead. At least they were talking instead of arguing. And at least her tension about the whole spider thing had eased. "As it gets closer to opening," he said, "and as Haven hires more people to work here, I want to do a people piece, too."

Had he thought Emma's tension had eased? Wow, was he wrong. At his comment about doing a people piece, her entire body seemed to seize up and her expression went right back to fearful.

"A people piece?" she echoed, the words coming out strangled and anxious.

He nodded cautiously. "Yeah. You know, talk to the people who were involved in Summerlight's renovation and the people who are going to be taking care of the place going forward." He grinned, hoping to disarm her again. "People like you."

Wow, had he thought she was only fearful? 'Cause now she was looking panicked enough to flee the premises— and him—right then and there.

"But you're not going to post that footage online, right?" she asked.

"What else would I do with it?"

She studied him in silence for a moment. Her fear did seem to ebb as she did, but she still looked uncomfortable. Then she told him, "I would prefer to not be included in that project."

"Why not?" he asked. "You're a key player. The first person Haven hired for Summerlight. You're helping complete the whole renovation. You're, like, the perfect interview subject."

"I am *so* not good for that."

He smiled. "Of course you are. You're cute," he told her without hesitation. Hey, it was true. "And you're smart. And funny. And articulate. You'd be a great selling point for this place."

She started shaking her head before he even finished talking. "I'm none of those things," she assured him.

"Oh, come on," he said.

There was no need for false modesty. Maybe Emma didn't go around citing a list of her assets all the time—or, you know, ever—but it couldn't possibly be news to her that she was all of the things he'd just said she was. All she had to do was look in a mirror and at how the people around her responded to her. Not just Pax, but Haven and Bennett, too. They clearly adored their new housekeeper.

"I don't want to be in any video footage," she told him flatly.

"Why not?"

"I just don't want to be a part of anything like that. Don't even include me in the background of any shots."

"Why not?" he asked again, since she hadn't really answered that question the first time.

"I'm just not comfortable being filmed," she told him. "Promise me you'll make sure I never appear in anything you put online. Ever."

His *uh-oh* radar went off again. Most people would have jumped at the chance to be included in a project like this. The whole fifteen-minutes-of-fame thing. And even if she wasn't someone to whom those fifteen minutes were important, she seemed like she cared enough about Summerlight to do whatever she could to make sure it was successful. Being filmed for something like this was no big deal.

He started to object, saying, "But—"

But she interrupted with, "Promise me, Pax. I mean it."

"Why?"

"I have my reasons."

"Would you like to share them?"

"No."

He waited for her to say more, but she only met his gaze levelly and left it at that. Pax challenged her for a few seconds, silent stare to silent stare, but she didn't back down.

Finally he said, "Okay, fine. You won't show up in any of the video I post about the inn."

"You promise?"

"I promise. Jeez."

She still looked a little mistrustful, but she said, "Thanks. I appreciate it."

The mood between them wasn't exactly what he had hoped for when he made the trip to Sudbury. He'd hoped maybe he and Emma could venture into town together and enjoy a late lunch or dinner somewhere again. That wasn't looking likely, though, with the way things were hanging between them.

"Well," he said. "I guess I'll just wander outside and look for something to shoot. If you can take a break for lunch or if you're not doing anything after you finish work and you feel like joining me for a trip into town…"

He left the statement unfinished. Mostly because he had no idea how to finish it. Today just felt so different from the last time he saw Emma. That night they spent on the dock talking had been so easy and comfortable.

They'd talked like old friends, as if they'd known each other for years. Today Emma felt like a stranger. A stranger who didn't like him very much, at that.

"I still have a lot of work to do," she said, as if to hammer that feeling home. "Not really gonna have time to break for lunch, and I'll probably have to work past dinner. Thanks anyway, though, for the invite."

Well, that certainly didn't allow room for anything happening between them today. "Sure," he finally said, the word coming out more clipped than he intended. "Anytime."

He couldn't see any reason to hang around, so he lifted a hand in a quick, impersonal farewell, then spun on his heel and headed for the ballroom's wide, arched exit. He was nearly through it when Emma called out after him.

"Pax?"

He stopped and turned around halfway. She was looking at him with her brows arrowed downward again, but this time she didn't look as if the reaction was because she didn't like what was going on. This time she looked like she wanted to say something but didn't know how to say it. Or maybe she wanted to say something she knew she shouldn't say. Or something she knew he wouldn't want to hear. Pax wished he knew how to make it easier for her. It would have helped if he'd had any idea what the hell was going on in her head.

"What?" he asked.

She opened her mouth, then seemed to change her mind. "Nothing," she finally told him. "Never mind."

Okay. He would give it no more mind today. In fact, he would give Emma no more mind today. She knew where to find him if she wanted him. But it was looking like that wasn't the case, in spite of the way they'd shared pieces of each other last weekend. Maybe he'd misread her. Maybe he'd completely mistaken what that night had been about. Maybe she'd just been being nice to him. Being polite. Being friendly. Maybe what he'd thought had been a near kiss had been…something else for her. Though what, he couldn't imagine. There weren't a lot of ways to misunderstand a kiss, near or otherwise. Especially when the other person kissed you, albeit chastely and innocently, a few minutes later. But maybe he had misunderstood. Somehow.

He lifted a hand again, then turned around and continued on his way. And did his best to empty his mind of Emma and what might or might not be.

Chapter Seven

She had almost told him the truth. About everything.

As Emma watched Pax disappear through the ballroom entrance, it was all she could do not to call out his name again and ask him to come back and then spill every detail about who she really was and what had really brought her to Sudbury and Summerlight. He had just looked so confused and hurt and angry—understandably so—that she had nearly just blurted it all out right there, consequences be damned. Maybe she still didn't know him well, but during the time they'd spent together, he hadn't seemed menacing or self-serving or untrustworthy.

He hadn't seemed *any of those things*, she told herself again. What a difference a little word could make. But that one little word was what had prevented her from telling him the truth before now, and it kept her safe again for a little while. Maybe she knew him better now than she had the first few times they were together, but that was just the point—they'd only been together a few times. Just because someone seemed okay didn't mean they were okay. Plenty of people seemed to be something they weren't. It was easy, especially in the early stages of getting to know someone, to present a front that seemed kind and charming and sweet. But it could be just that—a front. Everyone put on their best face when they were trying to make a good impression in the beginning. And then once they had the trust they sought from another, that best face could come off.

Pax had told her himself he'd been raised by con artists who made their living by pretending to be people they weren't. Even if he was living on the straight and narrow now, he'd gained the skill set at an early age that allowed him—encouraged him, even—to present a false persona specifically to take advantage of people. Maybe it had once been for financial gain and maybe he'd left that life behind, but who knew what he might be using those skills for now? He might not even do it consciously. It might just be second nature to him to present himself as something he wasn't until he gained someone's confidence. Hell, that was where the *con* part of *con artist* came from. She just couldn't quite bring herself to trust him with the truth. Not yet.

It didn't matter how kind and charming and sweet she found him. Or how hot and sexy and breathtaking. It didn't matter how much she had grown to like him or how he made her want to throw caution to the wind and be with him. She couldn't tell him who she really was. Not yet.

Though that had almost become a moot point, because while she'd been hopping around screaming about the spider, he'd come *this close* to seeing the tattoo on her back that would have outed her as Amber Finch the minute he saw it. Photos of her tattoo had shown up beside nearly every picture of her face online once

Travis Swope sicced his flying monkeys on her. The fact that her stomach pitched now at the very thought of Pax learning who she was by seeing it only hammered home how much she needed to keep her identity under wraps for a while longer. If the thought of him knowing who she really was made her feel physically ill, she was nowhere close to trusting him enough to tell him. She was going to have to be more careful with her spontaneous responses to him.

Oh, sure, that should be so *easy,* she thought wryly. Every time the guy entered a room, the entire room seemed to dissolve into nothingness around him. He was a man who commanded attention, and Emma was helpless not to give it to him. Jeez, whenever he came within eyeshot, she wanted to give him a lot more than just her attention. She wanted to give him her heart, her soul, the very essence that gave her breath. She wanted to give him a hand, give him a call, give him a sign, and any spare change in her pockets. She'd practically just given him the shirt right off her back just now. Spider dance aside—

And just where is that damned spider now? she wondered, looking around. Anything to take her mind off of Pax. She finally spied it halfway up the wall, about ten feet away from where she was standing. It had escaped without her or Pax even seeing it. Even so, she decided it was still way too close. She also knew that if she just left it alone, it would turn up in her bedroom later. Probably in her bed. While she was sleeping. Yeah, spiders were our friends and all that, despite their eight hairy legs and million beady eyes and proclivity for scaring

138   *KEEPING HER SECRET*

the bejeebus out of people and… She shuddered just thinking about it. She didn't have to be *their* friend. But she probably shouldn't kill it, either.

She knew that Haven, weirdly, had no problem with spiders. Or bugs or rats or snakes or any other kind of creepy-crawly. Still, that didn't mean they had to share Summerlight with any of them. Not the insides of the inn anyway. So Emma grabbed her phone from where she'd placed it on the floor by the ballroom's entrance— never once letting Mr. Spider out of her sight—and texted her employer about the situation, telling Haven she'd keep an eye on the creature while waiting for her to bring a glass to trap it and take it outside. No, a bucket. No, a garbage can. No, a U-Haul. No, an RV.

Okay, maybe it wasn't quite that big. It was big enough. Truly, it had seemed RV-size when it first landed on her. She shuddered again. Thankfully Haven came quickly and dispatched the creature—with her bare hands, no less, something that made her a goddess of primordial stature as far as Emma was concerned— then she went back to work. With a watchful eye on the walls and ceiling overhead for the rest of the afternoon, 'cause you never knew if there was a Mrs. Spider hanging around, too.

By the time she called it a day and started making her way through the inn to her bedroom, that long, golden light Pax had been talking about was at its prime, bending through the windows of Summerlight in a way that made her realize it was the reason for the house's name. Haven had told her a lot about Summerlight's history—that her great-great-lots-of-greats-grandfather Moreau, a robber baron right up there with the likes of Vanderbilt, Carnegie and Rockefeller, had initially built the house as an escape for his family when the summer heat of New York City became oppressive for all the layers of clothing they wore back in the eighteen hundreds. And how it had fallen into the possession of Bennett's family not long after that due to nebulous—read: contentious—reasons that had the two families feuding for generations, since neither really knew what those reasons were. Haven and Bennett themselves had been less than friendly when they first inherited the mansion together from his great-aunt under the condition that they share the residence for a year without one of them murdering the other in their sleep.

But all had become clear last fall after Haven found her great-great-lots-of-greats-grandmother Moreau's diary and discovered the truth—that Bennett's ancestor had saved the life of the Moreaus' toddler son, so they had gifted him the house as a reward. Apparently, giving away grand houses had been something robber barons could afford to do. But with no feud to keep Haven and Bennett apart—and having fallen for each other anyway, which had probably been Bennett's great-aunt's hope all along—the couple had learned to trust each other and ultimately embrace the same vision for the house.

They had learned to trust each other, Emma thought. The way Bennett's great-aunt had trusted them to do right by the mansion she'd loved. Trust seemed to be kind of an intrinsic feature to Summerlight. Emma wondered if it would work the same magic on her and Pax.

She continued on her way up to the fourth floor, which was simply a long garret with three tiny rooms on each side of the hallway aisle. Her room was at the far end, on the left, with an arched window beside it at the end of the hall. When she paused by her door, she looked out that window and saw Pax on the grounds below, phone in hand, taking a long, slow, panoramic shot of the lake and its surroundings. All of which were, of course, gorgeous, from the emerald of the trees to the sapphire of the lake to the topaz of the sun to the mottled opal that was the village on the other side. Emma still couldn't believe how lucky she had been to land in place of such beauty and light after so many months of living in ugliness and dark.

Pax, too, was a part of that light, she couldn't help thinking. There was no way she could deny that. Even if she still couldn't quite bring herself to trust him completely, she did trust him to a large degree. Maybe if the two of them spent more time together, she would trust him entirely. And even if she didn't, it was nice just being in the general vicinity of him. It had been a long time—too long—since she had been able to enjoy the company of another human being. Haven and Bennett were great, but they were her employers. And even if they hadn't been, they were busy with the inn and with each other, so she didn't really see much of them. Sitting with Pax on the dock last weekend, sharing so much of themselves with each other, had been the first time Emma had done that since...

Well, maybe since forever. Even her friends in Seattle hadn't known the details about her unhappy childhood and the wandering that brought her to that city
in the first place. They'd never asked, and she'd never
offered.

Pax hadn't asked, either. But Emma had offered anyway. That had to mean something.

Instead of turning the doorknob to go into her room,
Emma turned herself around and headed back down
the stairs to the first floor. Then to the front door. Then
outside. She found Pax by the gardens, still filming.
Haven had brought someone down from Rochester last
spring to help her plan the gardens and get them going.
Since then, she'd been paying various members of the
Sudbury Garden Club to come weekly to tend to it.
Once she hired a full-time groundskeeper, that would
fall under their job description, but that was still a ways
away, she'd told Emma. Even so, the garden had been
beautiful and productive ever since Emma's arrival
more than a month ago.

It was lush and beautiful now. No wonder Pax wanted
to film it. Beebalms and coneflowers hobnobbed with
foxglove and coreopsis in the flower section, while a
variety of tomatoes and peppers frolicked with zucchini
and eggplant on the kitchen garden side. She'd learned
a lot from Bennett about what was growing out here,
because it was kind of a hobby to him when he had time
for it, and she'd seen him pull a complete dinner out
of the garden on more than one occasion. Since Emma
was closer to the kitchen part of the garden now, the
air was rich with the scent of basil and rosemary and

spearmint. Her stomach rumbled in response, and she suddenly realized how hungry she was. Thanks to the spider terror that had spoiled her appetite for lunch, she hadn't eaten anything since breakfast.

Pax continued his panoramic sweep of the garden, his gaze focused entirely on his phone as he turned his body to film. He didn't stop until he had Emma in his frame, something that made him stop his panning. He didn't stop filming, though, something that made her automatically lift a hand to cover her face—even though, for one thing, it was too late and he'd already filmed her, and, for another, he'd already promised her that she wouldn't be included in any footage he posted online. It was an automatic reaction, one borne in the early days of her exposure as Litha Firefly. Every time she'd left her condo in Seattle, there had been a gaggle of Swope followers outside waiting for her, all of them lifting their phones to film her—despite her efforts at masking her appearance with hats and sunglasses—so that they could send the footage as an offering to their god in the hope of receiving some kind of recognition. The hand-lift had become automatic and essential for her self-preservation.

"Sorry," Pax said when he saw her reaction, dropping his phone back to his side. "Didn't see you there."

The splendid light of late afternoon worked its magic on him, too, she noted, bathing him in a gentle light that was nothing short of bewitching. The breeze danced with his dark hair, the sun staining both it and his beard with flecks of auburn. Even his clothes seemed to glow in the soft, gilded light. If she hadn't known better, she would have thought the garden had sprouted him, too, out of sunlight and flora and magic. In that moment, he just seemed too good to be true.

"It's okay," she said softly. And then, because she realized she hadn't greeted him properly, she smiled and added, "Hi. Sorry I didn't say that earlier."

He smiled back. "You're saying it now. Hi back."

"I'm sorry about earlier," she continued. "I didn't mean to be..." She expelled an errant breath. "Mean," she finally finished. "I didn't mean to be mean."

He shook his head. "You weren't mean. You were scared."

She nodded. "And when I get scared, I tend to react without even thinking. For that, I apologize."

Once again, she was telling him the truth. She did react without thinking when she was scared, which was why she was in her current predicament. Maybe if she had reacted more rationally when everything went to hell with Travis Swope and his fanboys, things would have turned out differently. Maybe if she'd stood her ground and defended herself—both online and in person—she wouldn't have had to go on the run. Maybe if she'd kept reporting the harassment and attacks until the authorities hadn't had any choice but to react properly, she could have nipped this whole thing in the bud before it got so horribly out of hand.

Then again, if she'd done any of those things, she might very well have been brutalized in the very ways she'd been threatened, over and over again. As an either-or situation, hers had sucked.

You did what you had to do, she told herself for perhaps the millionth time since going into hiding. *The only thing you felt like you could do.* Maybe her reaction to what happened to her ten months ago had been an overreaction. Maybe it hadn't. At this point, it really didn't matter. She was where she was, and she was doing her best. That was all she could do.

"You don't have to apologize," Pax told her. "A lot of people would have behaved the same way—or worse—if they were attacked the way you were."

Her stomach pitched for a moment when she thought he was responding to the very thoughts that had been tumbling through her brain. Thankfully he clarified, "You just never know what a spider is going to do."

She expelled a quick breath and hoped the relief that overcame her at that didn't show. "They're not trustworthy," she said.

He nodded in agreement. "They're totally not."

For another moment, they only gazed at each other in the luscious amber light of the waning afternoon. Emma had never been a particular fan of summer. She was much more of an autumn, and even winter, person. But looking at Pax now, in the light of this particular summer in this particular place, she could certainly see the appeal.

"Can I make it up to you?" she asked. "Fix you dinner before you head back to Ithaca? Haven and Bennett have given me free rein of the kitchen whenever I need it until the inn opens. And the garden, too. I was going to make myself some tomato soup and a grilled-cheese sandwich, but it would be no extra trouble to make enough for two."

"Tomato soup out of fresh tomatoes?" Pax said. "How can I say no to that? I'll even help you pick them."

They made short work of the task, with Emma doing everything she could to not notice how gentle, how attentive Pax was when he handled the delicate fruits. Really, she hardly noticed at all how he curled his fingers so carefully over the round bottom of a tomato; how he hefted its weight so reverently; how gently he caressed its tender flesh when he skimmed his fingers from one side to the other, from bottom to top; how his thumb raked so sensuously, so seductively along its—

"Emma?"

She looked up at the sound of her name, only half remembering where she was, because she had been so engrossed in such an intimate fantasy—*so* engrossed in *such* an intimate fantasy—that she could scarcely remember her name. But then who needed to remember one's name when one was being touched so erotically by such a sexy man, one whose fingers were working such wanton magic—not just on her breasts and belly but even lower, on her thighs and hips and between her...

Pax's dark eyes went even darker when he saw how she was looking at him. As hard as she had tried to keep her thoughts to herself, she clearly was *not* keeping her thoughts to herself. Also clear was the fact that Pax had been talking the whole time she'd been watching him pick tomatoes—and, um, nearly having a mental orgasm—while she hadn't picked any at all, because she'd been so wrapped up in his ministrations...uh, his handling of the tomatoes...and she had no idea what he'd been saying to her during his fondling...uh, his picking. But she did know she must be blushing, because she could feel the heat in her face and neck, and lower, too, in her chest and breasts and belly, and even lower between her—

Wow, was the summer sun hot today. Phew, could she use a glass of ice water. To pour all over herself.

Pax was still looking at her in a way that gave her the impression that he, too, was thinking about something other than picking tomatoes. He even seemed to be leaning in closer than he had been before, something that made her want to lean into him, too. And then wrestle him to the ground, dinner be damned. He looked at her more intently, his gaze moving from her eyes to her cheeks to her mouth. Emma realized in that moment that if she didn't do something quick, the two of them were indeed going to tumble to the ground right then and there and make love among the rhubarb.

So she hastily grabbed a couple of tomatoes herself and said "Okay, I think that's enough" and hoped like hell he thought she meant enough tomatoes and not enough, um, other stuff. Because, frankly, there hadn't been nearly enough of that.

Yes, there has! she immediately corrected herself. The last thing she should be thinking about was fondling anything with Pax.

This time he seemed to be the one who needed a moment to reel himself in, because he only continued to look at Emma as if she were the most delectable thing in the whole garden. Just for good measure—and to guide his attention elsewhere—she grabbed one more tomato and turned to head back into the house. On her way, she broke off a handful of basil, too. She really hoped Pax was following her, because she didn't dare turn around and look at him. Not until she could trust herself to keep hidden the thoughts still cartwheeling through her head.

Thankfully there was nothing like a kitchen full of dirty dishes in the sink to completely quash one's libido. Or, at least, mostly quash one's libido. Or quash it a tiny bit anyway. Emma should have checked in here before heading outside, because part of her job was ensuring that the kitchen was cleaned up following everyone's lunch. Haven and Bennett were always kind enough to at least rinse out their dishes when they were done, but it fell to Emma to fill—and ultimately run—the dishwasher whenever it was needed. So she decided to go ahead and do that before starting dinner, since, one, dishes in the sink were gross; two, it was her job—duh; and three, it just gave her more time to recover from the whole sexy-tomato-picking thing.

Or, at least, it would have if Pax hadn't offered to help. He did at least stay on one side of the dishwasher while Emma kept to the other, even when their hands kept bumping and tangling together and stirring up all her lascivious thoughts again. But when he offered to help her make dinner, too, she had to put her foot down. If they both started handling those tomatoes again, it wasn't just going to be love among the rhubarb around here. *Um,* making *love among the rhubarb*, she corrected herself. Because love itself was a whole 'nother thing. One that neither of them was in any way feeling for the other. *Right? Right.*

"No, I insist on making dinner solo," she told him. "It's my way of apologizing to you for my snippiness this afternoon. You sit. There," she specified, pointing to a chair in the farthest corner of the kitchen, as far from her person as he could get and still be within earshot. "And keep me company while I work."

He looked as if he was going to object, but maybe he, too, thought a little distance between them wasn't a bad idea. Their conversation flowed as Emma grabbed an onion and some garlic from the pantry, washed and cut up the tomatoes, then threw everything into a pot with vegetable broth and a little salt and pepper. She was not normally a good cook. She was not normally a cook at all. In Seattle, she'd lived on carryout and her microwave. Since going on the run, however, she'd had to become creative.

There had still been carryout from time to time, which was how she'd referred to the items she found in dumpsters. It hadn't been as bad as it sounded, because she discovered the very first time she went diving that restaurants and grocery stores in America threw out a staggering amount of perfectly good, untouched, still safely packaged food. She'd just had to rely on produce and nonperishables, since she usually hadn't had any way to cook things. Oddly, that had caused her to eat more healthily than she had at any other time in her adult life, because produce had been a section of the grocery store she never entered when she lived on her own. Her other "carryout" had been whenever she briefly found work in restaurant kitchens and been able to take home some of the food at the end of her shift. Not that her employers had fed her or anything, but customers had often left a good portion of their meals behind on their plates. Again, untouched. Half sandwiches or undisturbed pasta salad and, once, a glorious half rack of ribs still completely intact. Who didn't get a to-go box for a half rack of ribs? Still, it had been a bonus for her.

She'd never been a proud person, but being homeless and alone and scared, she'd lost every inhibition she'd had left. She'd done what she had to do to survive. Anyone else would have done the same. It had honestly taken her a while to get used to the fact that having free rein in the kitchen and garden here at Summerlight was a part of her pay package and that Haven and Bennett genuinely wanted her to feed herself well. So when Emma had seen a few old cookbooks in one of the kitchen cabinets, she'd learned how to make a few things for herself for dinner. She'd been surprised to realize she actually enjoyed cooking. It was yet another enlightening fact about herself that she'd discovered since going on the run.

She and Pax talked about everything and nothing while she made dinner, then talked about nothing and everything as they enjoyed their dinner together. Afterward, he helped her clean up again, right down to pushing the button on the dishwasher once it was full. Then Emma made coffee, and they retreated to the patio to enjoy what was left of the evening before Pax had to head home. This time, Emma told him point-edly, before it got dark.

"Okay, fine," he agreed as the sun began to sink low in the sky. "I'll head home after coffee. But only if you promise to come visit me in Ithaca next time."

Emma would love that. As much as she liked her current living situation, she had been itching to get out of Sudbury for a little while. Having been on the run for so long, she just wasn't used to spending so much time in one place. Not to mention she would love to see Pax's world and how he navigated it. There was just one problem: Ithaca was a big place. And a college town. Full of people who were no strangers to the inter-net. People who, in fact, thrived on the internet. People who—some of them anyway—were almost certainly followers of Travis Swope. And those followers might very well identify her as Amber Finch if they looked at her long enough.

She waited for the arrival of the chunk of ice that usually landed in her belly when she thought about the possibility of that happening. She waited to feel the dread and fear. Oddly, however, none of that happened. The thought of going someplace where she would be surrounded by people had terrified her for nearly a year. But now, thinking about visiting Pax in a place where that would be the case, she didn't feel frightened at all. How bizarre. Okay, so maybe there wasn't a problem with her visiting him in Ithaca after all.

Oh, wait—yes, there was, she realized when another one became obvious.

"I don't have a car," she reminded him.

"I'll come and pick you up."

She laughed. "You are not going to make a one-hour drive, one-way, just to have to turn around and drive us back another hour to Ithaca one-way and then do it again at the end of the day just to bring me home. That's silly."

She could, however, walk the mile to the nearest bus stop and take it to Ithaca. Which she told Pax she would be willing to do.

"That's a long haul, too," he said.

But it would be worth it. Maybe she could spend the night. Not with Pax, of course, but since it was a college town, there had to be affordable hotels all over the place.

"Are there any hostels in Ithaca?" she asked.

He looked surprised by the question. "Not that I know of, not officially anyway. But there might be. For sure there are plenty of places that offer cheap student lodging." When he finally understood what she was asking, he continued, "If you want to spend the night, you don't have to pay for a hotel. You can stay at my place. It has two bedrooms," he hurried on, obviously worried she might think he was suggesting something more intimate. "Though Cairo kinda thinks the spare room belongs to him."

His cat, she remembered. She'd heard they could be proprietary little buggers. Not that she had personal knowledge. Her parents had forbidden her from having a pet because they were too expensive. As an adult living alone, she'd never looked into adopting one herself. She just hadn't known anything about how to take care of one. What if she was a bad pet mom? It wasn't like she'd had any good examples to follow when it came to nurturing and loving and parenting.

But was it a good idea to spend the night at Pax's place? Yes, the two of them were definitely getting to know each other better, and, in some ways anyway, Emma did trust him. But they still didn't know each other *well*, and she still didn't trust him unconditionally. On the other hand, even staying in cheap lodgings would eat up a lot of what little money she'd managed to save so far. And she really was trying to keep as much money as she could in the top drawer of the dresser in her bedroom, in case she had to leave again at a moment's notice. Probably, that wasn't going to happen, though. Probably, she was safe here in Sudbury and would stay safe. Probably.

But maybe not.

"I don't mind sharing a room with Cairo," she finally told him. "As long as he doesn't mind sharing one with me."

When she realized she had just pretty much agreed to spend the night at Pax's place, she was more than a little surprised. She'd never spent the night with any guy before, platonic relationship or not. Even with guys she had dated for months, and guys with whom she had a bona fide relationship, she'd just never felt comfortable sharing a bed—or even a roof—with them overnight. Yet here she was, accepting an invitation from Pax, whom she'd only known a matter of weeks. Obviously she did trust him about that at least.

He smiled at her acceptance of his offer. "Great. When do you want to get together?"

Although Emma's schedule was pretty flexible until the inn's official opening, Haven was making a schedule for her every week, and Emma wanted to stick to it. She'd made her own hours when she lived and worked in Seattle, and it had been easy to slack off. Sometimes to the point where she got way behind in her work and had to scramble to make her deadlines. It had been another surprise to her to discover that she liked having a regular, specific schedule and actually had a work ethic. Strangely, having a schedule made by someone else had made her more productive than choosing her own hours had.

"My days off next week are Sunday and Thursday. I'd have to be back at Summerlight by eight the day after each if I want to be on time to start work at nine."

"I can be off Thursday and Friday both," he told her. "If you take the bus down on Thursday, we can get up early Friday and I can drive you back on time." When she started to object—surely there was a bus that left early enough to get her back here on time—he held up a hand to stop her. "That would give me a chance to do some morning filming of the inn for the videos. Catch it early, when the light is completely different."

A bead of something warm and pleasant bubbled up inside Emma, effervescing into a frothy happiness that spread to every cell in her body. She told herself it was only because she'd been the restless type since leaving home and could never sit still for long, and it would be nice to get out of town for a while and see and do new things. But really, she hadn't felt restless at all since coming to Summerlight. Since meeting Pax. No, lately, she'd kind of been feeling like she'd found a place where she could stay for a good, long while. Where maybe she could stop feeling restless completely, because it was a place where she could be content. Where she could belong. So if she was feeling happy in that moment, it was at the prospect of simply spending time with Pax. Truth be told, it didn't matter where they went. But it would be fun to see what his world was like.

"Sounds like a plan," she said. "Pretty sure the bus can get me to Ithaca in time for breakfast."

Pax smiled. "I know just the place."

Chapter Eight

Okay, okay, so the place Pax had known would be perfect for breakfast with Emma was actually a Cuban food truck that made its home not far from Cornell's campus. Its *café Cubano* was unbelievable, and its *pastelito de guayaba* was the food of the gods. Plus it was close enough to Sunset Park that he and Emma could enjoy their breakfast with a gorgeous view. It was already promising to be a perfect July day, with clear blue skies and mild temperatures and just enough of a breeze to stir the trees to life.

"This is nice," Emma said when they sat down on a bench overlooking Cayuga Lake. "But why is it called Sunset Park? That sounds like a place that would be on the West Coast, not the East Coast. A place like this seems like it should be Sunrise Park."

"Nah," he told her. "Sunrise at this park isn't anything out of the ordinary. Nice, but nothing out of the ordinary."

Emma surveyed their surroundings, then spared Pax an admonishing look. "Nice? Excuse me? This place is gorgeous."

He grinned. "Yeah, but it's even more gorgeous when

the sun goes down, since it goes down over the lake there and turns it into gold." Though he was thinking just then that the park this morning was indeed more beautiful than it normally was this time of day. But that was only because Emma was at the middle of it. It was pretty amazing at sunset, too.

She looked even more beautiful than usual today somehow. She was dressed in the same skirt and top she'd worn when they ran into each other that day in Sudbury and ended up sharing lunch. But where that day her hair had been unbound, today it was pulled back in a loose ponytail that was quickly surrendering strands to the morning breeze. And where that day she'd seemed a bit tense and closed off when he first sat down with her, today she was relaxed and open. *Happy*, Pax thought. That was how she looked. The first few times he'd encountered her, he hadn't quite been able to say that. Now he could. He wondered what had caused the difference and couldn't help hoping that maybe he'd had at least a small hand in it himself.

He'd taken care with his own clothing for the day, too—well, as much care as he ever took—opting for a pair of dark blue jeans and his favorite bowling shirt, this one black with a wide white stripe on the right and a trio of red diamonds over the left breast pocket. And, of course, his very nicest black high-top Converse.

Emma sipped her coffee as she looked around again, then sighed with much contentment. "It really is beautiful up here in this part of the country," she said. "I'd honestly never seen anything like it before coming to Sudbury."

Pax thought the statement odd. Although he'd never been to Altoona itself, he'd visited that part of Pennsylvania more than once. From what he remembered, it wasn't a whole lot different from this part of New York. Maybe there weren't any major lakes, but pretty much every city of any size had picturesque water views somewhere. And hadn't she mentioned that Altoona had a canal or something when they were talking about it before? He was about to ask her more about it, but she'd bitten into her guava pastry and was realizing it was indeed ambrosia and was giving him a look like *Why didn't you tell me about this so I could prepare myself?*

"Right?" he said, fully understanding her reaction. He remembered the first time he'd bitten into one of Señora Alvarez's *pastelitos*. "We can get some to go for breakfast tomorrow."

She nodded with much enthusiasm as she continued to chew, making little noises of delight that Pax assured himself were *not* sexual in nature. Those pastries really were just that good.

"We need to figure out how to get this truck to Sudbury," she said once her culinary orgasm subsided. "Not that I want to put Jack's or Dragonfly Café out of business, but maybe for a day or two."

"I know you're not being serious, but that gives me an idea," he said. "Food-truck week at Summerlight this time next year. Yet another way to bring in out-of-towners, even if for a day or two."

"I thought you were just their social media guy," she

said with a smile. "I didn't realize Haven had hired you for regular advertising and PR stuff, too."

He shrugged. "Social media, advertising and PR stuff. Kind of one and the same these days."

"Good point."

"Something to bring up to Haven anyway," he said. Now Pax was the one to smile. "You have some really good ideas," he told her. "Maybe Haven should hire you to do the inn's PR. You could even do a podcast or vlog about it. TikTok is perfect for that kind of thing."

Her smile fell, and her expression clouded. She dropped her gaze back to the pastry in her lap when she said, "Yeah, no. I don't think so."

"Why not?" he asked. "You'd be a natural on a platform like that. You'd have a million followers in no time."

She just shook her head. "I'm not good with stuff like that."

Pax found this hard to believe. Emma was one of the most natural, appealing people he'd ever met. Warm, unassuming, charming. Smart, funny, interesting. She was exactly the kind of person who would inevitably draw a crowd if she put herself out there. She'd made crystal clear that she didn't want to draw attention to herself or be the center of anyone's attention, but he still couldn't imagine why she felt that way.

"Suit yourself," he said. Half-jokingly, he added, "Maybe *I* should hire you, then. Or we could go into business together."

"No, thank you," she said, still not looking at him. "I'm not good with people."

The hell she wasn't. Maybe that first day she'd been overly wary around him, but since then she'd really come out of her shell. People responded to her in a way he hadn't seen people respond to strangers. Haven and Bennett obviously loved her. Marge, the server at Jack's, had treated like a favorite grandchild, even though she couldn't have met Emma more than a few times. And Señora Alvarez just now, after meeting Emma for the first time, had responded to her as if the two of them had known each other for years. Hell, Emma would give Pax's family a run for their money if she ever decided to go into the confidence game business, because her appeal was honest and not manufactured. She didn't have to pretend to be someone she wasn't to make others feel good around her. Where had her insistence on always being in the periphery come from?

When she looked up at him again, her expression had cleared, and her smile was back. "So what are we going to do today?"

"Depends," he said. "Do you want to be a tourist or a resident?"

"You've seen what a day in my life is like." She bobbed her head back and forth. "Well, how boring a day in my life is. Now I want to see what a day in yours is like."

If she thought her life was boring, she was going to be put to sleep by his. Somehow he didn't think inviting her to his minuscule office to watch him grade papers or work on course outlines or put together a proposal for *Popular Science* was what she had in mind.

So he conceded, "We can start with me showing you

around campus a bit, since it's nearby. I'll even show you my office and let you sit at my desk," he added magnanimously.

She laughed at that. "Ooh, thanks. Next time you're at Summerlight, I'll let you mop the foyer for me."

He chuckled, too. "But there's a lot more to Ithaca than Cornell," he told her. "I can show you some of my favorite places. And tonight, *I'm* cooking dinner for *you*."

She nodded once at that. "Sounds like the perfect day to me."

It did sound kind of perfect, didn't it? Weird, since as much as Pax liked living here, there were other places he'd liked more. He wouldn't call Ithaca perfect, as nice as it was. At least, he wouldn't have before today. Having Emma here to enjoy it with him, though, made it seem like the best place on the planet.

Although there were a lot of places in and around town to spotlight the beauty of its flora and fauna, after leaving campus—and yes, letting her sit at his super messy desk—Pax did indeed take Emma to all his favorite spots. They explored new releases at Buffalo Street Books. They had lunch at Moosewood Restaurant and dessert at Sweet Melissa's Ice Cream. They sampled Bordeaux at Ports of New York Winery and bought a couple of bottles to enjoy later—and they took the tour, too, which Pax had never done before. They drove past Cinemapolis so he could show Emma where he enjoyed the odd—sometimes very odd—movie. And they took in the vintage and thrift stores around Ithaca Commons since, like Pax, Emma loved those, too. Though where he was always drawn to the vintage and whimsical, Emma was clearly more attracted to items that were…um… He decided to call her taste *eclectic*. Yeah, that was a good way to describe the pairing of the hot-pink, many-zippered miniskirt and black lace tank top she came *this close* to buying.

He never would have guessed that under the peasant-skirt-draped earth-mother-goddess that was Emma Brown beat the heart of a punk-rock girl. He wondered how many other times she'd come *this close* to making purchases more suited to an audacious, in-your-face spitfire and curbed the urge. She assured him she wanted to keep a low profile, yet she was clearly drawn to brash, attention-grabbing fashion. The more time he spent with her, the bigger the enigma that was Emma Brown became. He was beginning to feel as if he were putting together a jigsaw puzzle for which there were a few pieces missing. Or maybe those pieces had just fallen off the table onto the floor—they were that close—if only he could find them to complete the picture and make it whole.

Their last stop on the One Day in Ithaca tour was the Ithaca Farmers Market so that Pax could pick up the makings for their dinner. He wasn't exactly ready to audition for *Top Chef*, but he didn't do too badly in the kitchen—especially if he wasn't in the kitchen at all but was actually out on the patio at the grill. Which he would be tonight, since, in case he hadn't mentioned it already, it was a perfect day. And not just with regard to the weather.

He grabbed a flat-iron steak, a couple of potatoes to stick in the oven and some salad greens to toss with a little homemade vinaigrette. Then they drove to his house in Cayuga Heights to kick back, relax and enjoy the rest of their night together. *Evening* together, he hastily corrected himself. He and Emma would not be spending the night together. Not in the same room anyway. Not yet.

"Of course you live in a mid-century-modern house," she said from the passenger seat the moment Pax put the car in Park.

"I got a great deal on it," he told her. "It was a wreck when I bought it, and I did most of the repair work myself."

She smiled. "Yeah, I saw the houses we passed as we drove here. Even as a wreck, this place couldn't have come cheap."

Busted, Pax thought. Then again, Emma should probably know the truth about him. The whole truth. Not just what he'd cherry-picked so far.

"Okay, I confess I didn't exactly leave home penniless," he told her after they exited the car. He looked at her over the roof. "When I told you how I come from a family with no scruples, that extended to me back then. I didn't have any either for a long time. Every time I ran a con with or for my parents, I skimmed some off the top for myself without telling them. And for every scam I ran for them on the Net, I ran another one for myself that they never knew about. One that usually made more money than any of theirs did. Sometimes my scams made a lot more than theirs did."

He waited for her to be repulsed by his unscrupulousness. Instead she only met his gaze matter-of-factly. "So you bought this place with your ill-gotten gains."

He blew out an exasperated—with himself—breath. "Yeah. Mostly, I did. Some of the money I came by honestly." Now he expelled an errant breath. "Okay, sort of honestly. Once I turned eighteen, I started investing my ill-gotten gains, and I invested very well. So that investment money was earned honestly. But the seed money for it, not so much."

He waited for her to reply to that, but she only gazed at him in clear expectation, knowing that wasn't the end of the story. Which, of course, it wasn't.

So Pax continued, "I was able to pay cash for this place by the time I bought it ten years ago. I used the rest of the money I had by then, along with a lot of elbow grease, to fix it up."

He waited for more disgust from Emma that he had benefitted so beautifully by his gross misdeeds. But no disgust ever came. At least, none that he could detect. She told him, "That was actually really good financial planning on your part." And damn if there wasn't even some admiration there.

He shook his head. "No way was anything I did as a kid admirable in any way," he assured her. "And if I could turn back time and reimburse everyone I ever stole from every nickel that I took from them, with interest, I would. But there's no way I could remember who any of those people are. And even if I could, there's no way for me to contact them now." He shrugged with a lot less concern than he was feeling. "It was a scummy thing to do. And I'm sorry I was involved in any of it."

"But it was how you were raised for more than half your life," Emma reminded him. "You didn't know any better."

"That doesn't make it any less scummy," he replied. "And there came a point when I did know better but just didn't care. And for that I'm sorry, too."

Emma continued to study him inscrutably. "So?" she finally said.

"So what?" he replied, confused.

"So I know you well enough to know you didn't leave it at that," she told him with absolute certainty. "Maybe you were raised to disregard the feelings of others, Pax, but you're not that way now. I know you've done something to make up for your past. You've made some kind of atonement for the things you did back then."

He didn't think he was that obvious. But he admitted, "Yeah, okay. I still make a lot from my investments. Once I got the house finished and started working as a TA—and thanks to my scholarships covering tuition—I really didn't need that much income. So now the entirety of my income from those investments goes to charitable organizations."

The ghost of a smile played about her lips. "What kind of organizations?"

He expelled another exasperated sound. "Organizations that take care of the elderly."

Now Emma's smile went full blown. "I knew it. I knew you would do something like that. You are so transparent, Pax."

There was a time when no one would have told him that. He had kept more secrets and lied so well that no one could have detected what he was truly thinking, ever. But Emma could see right through him now. Maybe Emma could have seen through him then, too. She seemed like the type of person who would be able to sniff out a liar from a hundred miles away. That was how honesty worked, he supposed. People who were genuine could tell the ones who weren't. That Emma recognized that in him now was actually really flattering.

"Come on," he said, tilting his head toward the house. "I'm gonna fix you the best meal you've ever had."

She laughed as she reached for the car's back door. "Shouldn't be too hard to do, considering how I've been eating for the last—" She halted as abruptly as her laughter did. Then she smiled again. Though not quite as happily as before. And all she said was "Can't wait."

And then the puzzle that was Emma Brown grabbed the overnight bag from the back seat on her side. Pax grabbed the bag of groceries on his side, and they headed toward the front door. But he couldn't quite shake the feeling that as honest as she was, there was still something about her that Emma kept to herself. Not that he had a problem with that—people were entitled to their secrets. He just hoped someday she would feel comfortable enough to share at least a few of those with him, too.

The inside of Pax's house was as retro as the outside, Emma saw the moment she stepped through the front door. Although she hadn't seen a lot of old movies, she'd seen enough to know Pax's place could be used for the set on one of them. The snug one-story had an open concept, the midnight-blue living room on one side abutting a maple-clad kitchen on another, both attached by a wall of nearly floor-to-ceiling windows and a sliding door that opened onto a creek-stone patio. Creek stone, too, was the fireplace on yet another wall, whose mantelpiece sported the sort of classic bric-a-brac that might be found in someone's grandmother's house—a retro cocktail set, candlesticks and vases of weird op-art shapes—with, inescapably, a metal star-burst clock hanging above it. The artwork consisted of framed movie posters, all noirish in nature, and the rugs spanning the hardwood floor had space-age geometric designs.

As she took a few more steps inside, she saw that a short hallway ran past the kitchen, emptying into a trio of rooms she assumed were the bathroom and two bedrooms Pax had said he had. He guided her toward one of those so she could stow her overnight bag, and it was just as steeped in the mid-twentieth century as everything else in the house, from the curvy rattan furnishings to the abstract-grid-work art prints. Ditto for his room and the bathroom, the former having more of a space race theme that was filled with curves and starbursts, the latter teeming with mid-century-modern fish.

Emma would have sworn she would never have found anything retro or nostalgic charming. Her condo in Seattle had been the epitome of forward-thinking design, sleek and modern, angular and taupe. But she had to admit that Pax's place was infinitely cozier than her own.

Well, formerly her own. By now, someone else must be living there and making it *their* own. She had no idea how long foreclosure took, but she would guess that completely ghosting the mortgage lender and disappearing from the face of the earth had probably sped the process along even more than usual. The bank must have seized and resold her place by now. God only knew what had happened to her furniture and other possessions. Emma hadn't dared do too much digging or contact any of her friends in Seattle for fear that even those small things might jeopardize her whereabouts and reveal them to someone still looking for her. But that was what happened when you had to skip town and change your identity and ignore your debts. You lost everything.

She was just happy she was beginning to find a few things again. No material possessions, but things that were infinitely more valuable. A sense of perspective. An appreciation for things she'd taken for granted before. New friends. New likes and loves. Pax. Even herself.

"I like your place, Pax," she said with much understatement as she settled her bag on the bed.

"Thanks," he replied. "I did my best to keep it all authentic."

Which couldn't have been cheap, since, from what she understood, mid-century modern had been making a major comeback among people their age and was in huge demand. He really must be doing okay financially to live a life like this. So maybe he wouldn't be tempted even by a six-figure bounty placed on a certain someone's head by a certain scumbag on the internet.

And ding went another deposit into the ATM for Pax's good-guy account. Emma was fast running out of reasons not to trust him completely.

Although there was a time not too long ago when, even without confidence games and wise investments, Emma's income had probably rivaled his own, she hadn't been nearly as wise with her money as he had. Okay, okay, she'd been a complete spendthrift. She'd done without so much as a child that she'd gone a little crazy when the money from her security work started pouring in. Yes, she'd saved for the future—a little— but she'd mostly lived in the here and now.

Not that it mattered after everything that had happened. Having her finances hacked so thoroughly by Travis Swope's dirtball army, she would still be broke now, regardless of how much money she might have saved in any kind of account. Small comfort that she'd at least been able to enjoy some of her money by spending instead of some sycophantic little prick stealing even more from her.

She and Pax chatted softly as they returned to the living room, where, clearly alerted by the sound of their voices, a massive black cat had sauntered in from somewhere to jump up onto the back of the chocolate-brown tuxedo sofa. Instead of being aloof, however, he strode across the back of the couch to where Emma was standing. Then he bumped his head against her arm in a way that could only be described as affectionate, despite the fact that he nearly knocked her over when he did it.

"Mao," he then greeted her. Because he truly did seem to be addressing her as the former chairman of China.

"You must be Joel Cairo," she said.

"Cairo, meet Emma," Pax said to his pet. His friend. His pet friend. Whatever. "Emma, this is Cairo."

Cairo continued to look at her expectantly. Emma had no idea how to reply. Then he called her Chairman Mao again.

"He's expecting some pets," Pax told her.

Pets? she echoed to herself. How could a pet have pets? Oh, right. Pets as in being petted. But plural? As in he wanted more than one? She honestly wasn't sure she knew how. Or if she even should. The only cats Emma had ever encountered had belonged to friends, and none of them had seemed to like her. Or, at least, they'd never hung around when she went to said friends' houses. Cairo seemed to want to get to know her better.

Gingerly, she lifted a hand and began to move it toward him. The minute she did, Cairo lurched forward until his head was under her palm, moving around in a way that did the petting for her. Obviously he knew what was what and wanted to show Emma how it was done. Instinctively, she curled her hand and scratched the top of his head with her fingertips, only to be met by Cairo's rumbling, happy reply.

"Oh! He's purring!" she cried with delight.

Pax had been watching their tentative meeting with a smile, but now he looked at her incredulously. "Have you really never been this close to a cat before?" he asked.

"I mean, I have," she said. "Kind of. Friends of mine have had cats. But they've never really warmed up to me like this."

"I find it very hard to believe that there's anyone on this planet who wouldn't warm up to you the minute they met you."

Oh, if he only knew. Best to change the subject.

"So what can I do to help with dinner?" she asked. She tried to drop her hand from Cairo's head, only to have the cat duck beneath it again to insist on more pets.

He grinned. "If Cairo will let you, you can open the wine and pour us both a glass."

"I know how to do that," she said, grinning back. And continuing to scratch Cairo's ears, since he now had a paw on her hand to keep it there.

"I know you do," Pax said. "According to Haven, you once worked as a bartender."

Jeez, had Haven given Pax her entire fake résumé to memorize? Emma had heard small towns could be gossipy, but considering Haven had grown up on Staten Island, it sure hadn't taken her long to succumb to village life in Sudbury.

"I did," she said.

Honestly, too, since she'd pulled a bartending stint at a restaurant in Sedona one summer before moving to Seattle. The only manufactured job experience on her résumé had been the part about working as a hotel housekeeper, since she'd wanted to have something on there that would make her look like an appealing candidate for the position at Summerlight. The million other jobs had all been totally legit. She'd just sited them all on the East Coast instead of the West to keep her identity as Emma Brown of Altoona more credible. Even though her identity as Emma Brown wasn't exactly, um, credible.

They sipped their wine and chatted as Pax did the prep work for dinner, then they moved outside to wait for the grill to heat and chatted some more. He turned on the outdoor speakers and tuned his phone to what he called his grilling playlist, one filled with jazzy saxophones and hot drum solos and women singing about men who done them wrong. Between that and the house Pax called home, she felt like two generations had melted away and she was back in the days of big bands and black-and-white movies. She was really beginning to like this world that Pax lived in.

"So Mrs. Aebersold taught you about all this stuff," she said, recalling his story about his youth.

"Yep," he said. "And a whole lot more, too. Before I met her, I wasn't really into anything. Like I said, I read a lot, but I read everything I could get my hands on, not one thing in particular. She's the one who gave me a pile of paperbacks that belonged to her dad and told me I'd like them. Sam Spade and the Thin Man and Philip Marlowe. I still have a bunch of them. I'll loan you some."

Emma smiled. "I'd like that."

"And the music," he added enthusiastically, gesturing into the air around them, which was filled with big band music. "Man, I probably never would have heard any of this stuff if it wasn't for her. Now I can't get enough of it."

Emma smiled. "Okay, maybe you're not a ninety-eight-year-old man like I thought that day at Jack's," she said, recalling their first afternoon together. "But I bet you were a gumshoe in a previous life. Or maybe the saxophone player in a big band."

He sighed. "Either of those things would be very cool." He looked over at her. "So what do you think you were in a previous life?"

Emma thought about that. In order to determine one's previous lives, one really needed to have a specific proclivity that might lend itself to one of those lifestyles. Considering her two biggest strengths were cyber-hacking and cosmetics, she might have been someone like Ada Lovelace or Max Factor. Not that she could reveal either of those to Pax without also hinting at her true identity. But there must have been *someone* from the past she could have fittingly been...

Nope. She couldn't think of anyone.

"I have no idea," she finally told him. "I don't think I was anybody. I don't have an old soul like you do. Maybe this is my first life."

One she was still trying to pin down. Tough to identify past lives when you weren't even sure about this one.

"Everybody is somebody," he assured her. "You'll figure it out."

He said it with such confidence that Emma almost believed him. Maybe she would figure it out someday. Once all the chaos of this whole Travis Swope thing blew over. Because it would have to blow over at some point. It had to.

"Have you thought anymore about contacting Mrs. Aebersold?" she asked him.

"I have thought about it again since you mentioned it," he admitted. "But I still don't think it's a good idea. I mean, I was like a grandson to her. She even called me by his name a couple of times by mistake. That's how much I reminded her of him, and that's how much she came to care for me. She trusted me completely. And if I hadn't come to my senses, if I'd gone through with my parents' plan… It would have been like stabbing her right in the heart, Emma. If I hadn't finally realized what a kind, decent person she was and how she loved me more than my own family did…"

He made a sound that told Emma just how very disgusted with himself he was to this day.

"You recognized that because you were kind and decent, too," she told him.

He shook his head. "I lied to her for months."

"Only because you didn't know any better."

"That doesn't excuse it. Nothing excuses lying. Nothing."

Emma had to literally bite her lip to keep herself from saying anything more about it. Pax had made up his mind a long time ago that liars deserved nothing but contempt. She wished she could have a conversation with him tonight, right now, that would show him how things weren't that simple and how many things in life weren't a case of either-or. But it was a beautiful evening, and they were having a lovely time. She didn't want to mess that up. There would come a time that was right for her to tell him the truth about herself.

The whole truth. Because she was determined now to do that. But tonight, she just wanted to be with him in a way that was as uncomplicated as possible. Tonight was for the two of them to enjoy.

She did everything she could to keep the topic of conversation light and inconsequential after that, and she succeeded admirably if she did say so herself. Dinner, too, went swimmingly, conversation-wise, especially after Cairo joined them at the table. He sat in the chair across from Emma as he made conversation with them that mostly consisted of different cat sounds, all of them clearly requests for food. Pax reminded the cat that he did *not* get table scraps, which was clearly untrue, thanks to the cat's obvious comfortableness at the table.

Emma was surprised by Pax's lie, until he added the qualifier *when we have guests*, whereupon she realized he wasn't lying after all. She also realized that the admonition didn't deter Cairo, because the cat only turned to Emma alone, requesting that she—or possibly Chairman Mao, she still wasn't sure—was welcome to toss him a bit of steak or buttered potato or anything else she might not need from her plate. Then she and Pax cleaned up the remains of dinner, opened another bottle of wine—*No, Cairo, you may* not *have a sip*—and retreated to the living room to watch Pax's favorite film, *Casablanca*, which Emma had never seen.

The whole evening just felt so…normal, she couldn't help thinking as it passed. At least what must be normal for normal people. People who had grown up with a healthy home life and enjoyed a lifestyle that wasn't fraught with things like lying about who one was and being on the run and fearing for one's life. Though even before all the lying, running and fear, Emma couldn't really say her life in Seattle had felt normal. *Normal* suggested a complacency with life in general and with oneself in particular. And she could say honestly that she had never felt particularly complacent in either of those areas.

At least she hadn't before tonight. But with Pax, she did feel complacent. Though not in a bad way at all. She felt peaceful with him. Safe. As if she would never have to look over her shoulder at what lurked in the shadows or was creeping up behind her. As if she would never have to fear for whatever the future held. She didn't think she had ever felt that way before. It was nice. Kind of unsettling in a way, since she wasn't used to it, but nice.

Maybe the unsettled part was just because she hadn't quite surrendered the last few traces of mistrust she still felt around people. Not just Pax, but Haven and Bennett, too. Yes, she had come a long way since arriving in Sudbury six weeks ago. She no longer jumped every time she heard a strange sound that *might* be a person approaching, and she no longer felt the impulse to flee whenever a person did get too close. She had learned to laugh again and was allowing herself to feel more comfortable. She was beginning to like the way things were. But there was still enough of the last year's apprehension simmering beneath the surface—admittedly, though, not as deeply or as ingrained as before—to keep her from giving up that wariness completely.

Soon, she told herself. Every day brought her closer to believing she would be safe once the truth was out and that everything would eventually work out in a way that would allow her to live a normal, happy life from that point onward. Soon she would confide in the people around her. All of the people around her—Haven and Bennett and all the acquaintances Emma had made in Sudbury, but most especially, Pax. Soon she would tell him the truth about everything. If he really was someone she could trust—and she had come to the decision now that he was indeed someone she could really trust—he would understand. And even if he at first didn't react favorably, he would ultimately come to understand why she had behaved the way she had, and he would forgive her for the lies she had been forced to tell him.

Just not quite yet. Not tonight. She and Pax had spent such a lovely day together, and the night was promising to be just as enjoyable. It was too nice a night for her to do anything that might risk messing it up. Soon she would reveal the whole truth to him. Very, very soon.

Just not quite yet.

Chapter Nine

It was after midnight when *Casablanca* ended with Rick assuring Ilsa they'd always have Paris and telling Louis it was the beginning of a beautiful friendship. Emma wiped the tears from her eyes for the former and smiled about the latter. And she couldn't help thinking that she and Pax would always have Ithaca and it was the beginning of something beautiful for them, too. She just hoped neither of those things ever changed.

"Yeah, that's kind of how I felt about it, too, the first time I saw it," Pax told her. He thumbed the remote to turn off the TV, then took off his glasses and set them on the coffee table. "It's one of the best endings in cinematic history."

"Are all old movies like this?" she asked. "I've actually only seen a few, but none of them made this big an impression."

"Well, we're just going to have to rectify that situation ASAP," he told her. "And no, not many of them can compare to *Casablanca*. But a lot of them are really good. Next time, we can watch *The Maltese Falcon*. Humphrey Bogart again, but this time with Mary Astor. And Peter Lorre is in it again, too. In fact, he plays one

of the antagonists I named Joel Cairo after. Though that
Cairo—" he pointed to the cat who had been sleeping contentedly for the better part of the movie, on a
low bookshelf beneath a window facing the patio "—is
only antagonistic when he doesn't get dinner scraps. Or
enough pets. Or when I'm trying to work on my laptop.
Or when there's only half a bowl of kibble instead of a
whole bowl. Or when the woodpecker shows up in the
sycamore tree out front."

Emma was laughing by now. Pax only shook his
head at the softly snoring cat.

"Okay, maybe that Cairo is even more antagonistic
than the Peter Lorre one," he admitted. "He's still my
favorite of the two." He looked at her and smiled. "Anyway, *The Maltese Falcon* is a bit different from *Casablanca*. But I think you'll love it, too. It's arguably the
standard for all film-noire movies."

Film noire. His favorite, she remembered. Emma
loved that he wanted to share his favorite things with
her. She wished she could share her favorite things with
him, too. But going into depth with her knowledge of
all things tech related would risk revealing who she really was. And she was going to go out on a limb and
assume he probably wouldn't be all that interested in
the latest lipstick shades from MAC or how to shadow
his jawline to make his cheekbones more prominent.
Especially since his beard covered both. Then again,
she hadn't much kept up with the latest tech or cosmetic trends over the past nine or ten months anyway.

Strangely, though, thinking about them in this moment, she realized she didn't much care what was going

on with them now. Makeup was fun. And tech was always changing. But, understandably, neither of those had been a passion for her for some time. Thinking about them in this moment, she kind of felt like they were never really her *passions* to begin with. They were just things she was good at—very good at—and it had taken her a long time to find something she excelled at. Over the past year, though, she'd begun to realize she was good at a lot of other things, too. Things she never would have given a thought to before so never would have even tried. And she liked a lot of those things she'd never thought she would like before. Reading a lot of different kinds of books in a bunch of new genres while hiding out in libraries, for instance. She'd had no idea she would love historical fiction until she picked up a copy of *The Alienist* and then went looking for more books like it. Or cooking, first short-order dishes to earn a buck on the run, then leisurely dinners at Summerlight for her own enjoyment. Or mending her own clothes when they'd gotten messed up, something that had led to an interest in learning to sew, which she still wanted to pursue but could only look at tutorials on for now.

There had just been things emerging out of Emma's brain and spirit she'd never realized were there before. If nothing else, this whole Travis Swope debacle had made her realize she wasn't the person she'd been brought up to be or led to believe she was. She wasn't the unwanted, unloved child her parents had been forced to tolerate, and she was more than the tech genius and makeup maven she'd thought were her only strong suits.

Now she was discovering she loved old movies, too. *And cats*, she added to her mental list as Cairo stretched and rose from his sleeping spot, then sat on the shelf like some Egyptian feline deity to gaze upon both of them. She was still learning new things about herself. She was still emerging from the old Amber Finch into something new and different. She wondered how long it would be before she stopped emerging and finally materialized. And she wondered who she would end up being when that finally happened.

She had no idea. But she discovered she was liking this new person beneath her skin. Certainly more than she'd liked the one who left Seattle almost a year ago. Cairo seemed to agree, because he leaped down from the shelf and ambled over to the sofa, jumping up to crawl into Emma's lap without even asking permission. Clearly he knew she would welcome his presence. And, of course, she did. The rumble of a cat's purr, she was realizing, went a long way toward easing a person's anxiety. Big pharma could learn a thing or two from Joel Cairo.

"You know," Pax said as he watched the cat settle more snugly into her lap, "you might just have to sit there forever. When he gets that comfortable with someone, he never wants to move."

She scritched Cairo softly behind one ear, and he nestled even closer. "Does he get this comfortable with a lot of people?" she asked.

She was *not* asking about any other girlfriends Pax might or might not have had in the past. She wasn't. She was just curious, that was all.

Pax smiled in a way that told her he knew exactly what she was fishing for. Except he was wrong, because she totally wasn't fishing for anything. She wasn't.

"Actually, no," he told her. "Cairo is a very friendly guy, but it usually takes a while before he does the nap-in-the-lap thing." He looked at Emma again, his gaze fixed on her. "And if you're also asking about something else as well, the answer is no, I don't bring a lot of women home with me."

Emma gaped at him in a way she hoped conveyed her total, stark astonishment that he would ever think she could entertain such thoughts, but which was probably completely unconvincing. "I wasn't asking that at all," she told him. "You could bring home a different woman every night if you wanted to. That is totally none of my business."

He actually chuckled at that. "Whew, that's a relief. Because I already have three inked in for next week."

She swatted his shoulder, both of them laughing now. "Fine," she said. "But I bet Cairo won't nap in any of their laps."

Pax was still grinning. "He doesn't nap in anyone's lap but mine. And now yours," he amended. He hesitated a telling moment before adding, "I've never brought any woman home with me, Emma. Not until today."

This she found hard to believe, and she told him so.

He shrugged. "I'm just not usually comfortable spending the night with people," he said. "I never have been. Maybe it's because I had to share a room with so many cousins growing up. I never had a bed to myself until I left home. Or maybe it's because…" He dropped his gaze to the blissfully purring lump in her lap. "Maybe it's just that I've never been that—" he pointed to the sleeping cat "—comfortable with anyone enough to spend the whole night with them."

Emma understood completely. "I know what you mean," she told him. "I feel the same way. And I don't have the excuse of overcrowding. I never had to share a bed with anyone my whole life. But I've never liked spending the night with anyone, either."

"Guess that makes us two of a kind," he said.

"Guess it does."

They continued to study each other in silence for another moment, then, without warning—or maybe there had been plenty of warnings that Emma had done her best not to acknowledge—he dipped his head toward hers. She told herself to stop the kiss, that kissing Pax would only further complicate a life that was already way too complicated. Because she knew if she kissed Pax, it wouldn't be enough. It would never be enough. If she kissed Pax, she was going to want a lot more than kissing. It had been too long since she'd been with anyone. Too long since she'd shared the closeness of another human being. Too long since she had exchanged even a simple, physical touch. Too long since she had felt wanted or needed or loved—or whatever passed for love sometimes, when she just needed to be with *some*one. Too long.

Much, much too long.

Which was why she didn't stop the kiss. Which was why she lifted her head to meet him halfway. Maybe Pax didn't love her, and maybe she didn't love him.

Maybe. But she wanted him. She needed him. And in that moment, she couldn't think of a single reason why they shouldn't have each other.

His mouth touched on hers tentatively at first, a soft brush of his lips, once, twice, three times, four. Then he pulled back a little to meet her gaze, as if making sure he wasn't overstepping and that she wanted this as much as he did. In reply, she lifted her hand to his face, covering his jaw with sure fingers, loving the silky feel of his beard beneath her palm. She'd kissed men with beards before, and although she'd never minded the extra furriness, she hadn't been all that crazy about it, either. She preferred skin-to-skin contact, especially beneath her fingertips. But with Pax, the bristliness was actually kind of…well, kind of arousing. An added layer to the walking, talking turn-on that was Pax Lightfoot.

As if the thought had given her hand ideas, she dragged her fingers softly downward, over his cheek, his jaw and the strong column of his throat, to trace the elegant divot at its base. Her gaze followed her fingers until it fell to the top of his shirt, open enough to reveal the first part of his word tattoo that had so intrigued her during their lunch at Jack's that day a month ago. As if of its own free will, her hand dropped lower still to his collar, and she nudged aside the soft fabric so that she could see more. Buttoned up the way it was, though, she could still see only the first two words: *Down these.* She traced her index finger over both of those, then dropped her hand to the first button of his shirt, lifting her eyes to look at his before opening it.

Pax had followed her movements with his own gaze

and studied her intently now. Instead of nodding his assurance that it was okay for her to explore, he unbuttoned the first two buttons of his shirt himself. Emma pushed aside the garment to reveal the tattoo in its entirety, then read the words aloud.

"'Down these mean streets a man must go who is not himself mean.'" She met his gaze again. "Don't tell me—let me guess. Raymond Chandler."

He grinned, nodding. "Yeah. From an essay, not a novel, but it still hit home when I read it. There's, like, three paragraphs to the whole thought, but that would have left me in the tattooist's chair for a week. And the first sentence conveys the whole gist of it."

"I take it you thought of yourself as the man when you got it."

He nodded.

"I'm glad you were thinking of yourself as a man who *isn't* mean by then. Because you're not mean, Pax. You never were."

His expression was impenetrable, but his eyes were dark and hard. "I was once upon a time."

She shook her head. "No, you weren't," she said adamantly. "If you had been then, you'd still be traveling with your family, hurting people."

He studied her in silence for another moment, as if, even after all these years, he was still torn by what he was once and what he was now. Emma couldn't stand the thought of him entertaining, for even a moment, any idea that he wasn't a good person. He was a good person. The best kind of person. Certainly the best person she'd ever met.

She tried to scoot closer to him, then remembered she had a lap full of cat. Who had at least woken up by this point, but Cairo was only looking at both of them as if he couldn't believe they were more interested in each other than in him. Finally surrendering to his realization, though, he leaped down to the floor and headed off to be alone in his indignity.

Sorry, Cairo, Emma thought as she watched him leave. She'd make it up to him later. Honest she would.

Then she did scoot closer to Pax, cupping his cheek in her hand again and tilting her head toward his. This time Emma was the one to kiss him, but it was just as tentative, another soft brush of their mouths against each other, over and over again. Her heart raced in her chest like a wild animal, pumping heat into every part of her body. Soft brushes turned into intent kisses, with Emma looping one arm around Pax's neck as he roped one of his around her waist. After that the kisses went feral, each of them doing their best to consume the other and giving as good as they got.

She threaded her fingers through his silky hair, cupping the crown of his head to pull him closer, even though they were already as close as two people could be. He tucked his hand under the hem of her shirt and splayed his fingers wide over the small of her back, pulling her more intimately against himself. For a long time, they only necked and devoured each other, their hands wandering over everything they could reach. Emma finished unbuttoning his shirt and pushed it open, skimming her fingers over every salient muscle on his torso, then moved to his back, too, exploring the hot, silky skin she encountered there. Pax drove his hand over her hips and thighs, curling it under her fanny to pull her into his lap, and then...

Oh, *then*. Still kissing her, he tucked his hand under the front of her shirt, dragging his thumb along the lower curve of one breast before covering it completely with his palm. She gasped at the contact, and he took advantage of her open mouth to kiss her more deeply, then gently fingered her nipple, rousing such a furious hunger inside her that she had to pull away from his mouth to catch her breath. When she did, he lifted the front of her shirt and moved his mouth to where his fingers had been. She'd always thought she had small breasts and so never bothered with a bra, but Pax filled his hand with her and pushed her more deeply into his mouth, sucking her, licking her, stirring even more need in her with every move he made.

She was so focused on the havoc his mouth was wreaking on her breasts that she barely noticed when his other hand began pushing her skirt up over her thighs. Not until he urged her body backward until she was lying flat on the sofa and he could position himself atop her did she realize how far—and how fast—things were moving. Not that she cared. She wanted this—she wanted Pax—more than she'd wanted anything for a very long time. Maybe forever. If this first time was fast and furious, they could go slower next time.

He seemed to be of the same mind, because he moved his hand to her panties and began tugging them down. Emma helped as much as she could, lifting her hips as he pulled, then gasping at the obvious evidence of his arousal against her. As he tossed her panties to the floor, she fumbled with the zipper of his jeans until it was open and drove her hand inside. She found him immediately, heavy and hard, then wrapped her fingers around his stiff shaft to free it, caressing him from its base to its head and back again. As she stroked him, he found the hot core of her, too, burying his fingers in the damp folds to fondle her just as intimately. Again and again, his fingertips found more sensitive parts of her, until Emma's breath was as erratic as his own. He slid a finger inside her, then slowly withdrew it, then penetrated her again, this time more deeply. A second finger joined the first, then a third. She bucked her hips against him, pulling him even deeper inside.

Then, without warning, Pax repositioned himself on the sofa until he was on his knees beside it, turning Emma's body until he could taste the part of her he'd been teasing for so long. She cried out at the touch of his tongue against her, at the scrape of his beard on her sensitive thighs, her entire body convulsing at the contact. Then she tangled both hands in his hair, at once trying to divert his attentions so that she could catch her breath and ensuring that he would never leave her side. Over and over he enjoyed her, until she felt the crest of an orgasm curling inside her.

He seemed to realize how close she was to climaxing, because he stopped long enough for her to collect herself, moving back up onto the couch until she was lying prone beneath him again. She felt him at the apex of her thighs, still as hard as a rock, and she somehow found the presence of mind to capture him in her fingers again. He groaned at the contact but moved his hips to push himself more intimately against her fingers. She stroked him gently, then more insistently, until the head of his shaft was as damp and hot as she was. Then he wrapped his hand securely around her wrist to halt her and met her gaze levelly.

"Are we really going to do this?" he rasped.

She was fairly panting but somehow managed to reply, "Not sure how it escaped your notice, but I'm pretty sure we already are."

He was breathing heavily, too. "We haven't gotten to the main event yet. Are you sure?"

She nodded emphatically. "Yes. I'm very sure."

He nodded. "Me, too. But I have to go get a condom."

She shook her head. "No, you don't. I have an IUD."

He looked ready to dive right into her at that. She actually shuddered with anticipation.

Then he reminded her, "But there are other considerations."

STDs. The bane of twenty-first century life. But Emma knew she was okay, because she hadn't been with anyone for over a year. And Pax... Well. She trusted him now. He was as good a guy as any she'd ever known. Better than any guy. He was the best.

"I trust you," she told him. "And I haven't been with anyone myself for more than a year."

He smiled at that. "I trust you, too."

She had a moment of doubt. His assurance almost made her put a stop to what was happening between them. He trusted her as Emma Brown. Not Amber Finch. She was still misrepresenting herself to him about that. Still lying to him. But, she reminded herself, she'd been honest about everything else. He could trust her about that. And she was being honest with him in this, too. Her feelings for him now were the truest feelings she'd ever had. For anyone.

She smiled back. Then she moved her hand along his hard shaft again. He closed his eyes and exhaled a shaky breath. She stroked him again. He sighed. And sighed again. Somehow he grew even harder against her palm. By now the front of her skirt was up around her waist and her shirt was nearly up to her neck. Normally she would have at least removed that latter. But even though she was on her back, she couldn't risk him seeing her tattoo. Not until after she'd told him who she was and they'd had time to talk about it.

Then again, she couldn't help thinking, it was kind of erotic, the thought of making love while still nearly fully dressed. She pushed his jeans down farther over his thighs, then took him in her hand again. Then she spread her legs wider and guided him toward her. He braced himself with one hand on the back of the sofa and the other on the cushion beside her head, then pushed himself inside her. Slowly at first, gently, until he was buried completely. Emma sighed at the feeling of fullness that overcame her. His body in hers this way made her feel more complete than she ever had before. As if a part of her had been missing before Pax and now, at last, she was whole. He pulled out slowly, too, gently, then entered her again more boldly to go even deeper. Then he withdrew again and drove himself inside her once more.

Again and again, he thrust against her, and again and again, Emma felt as if she were coming home. But it still wasn't enough. She wanted to feel him deeper still. As Pax sensed that, he moved their bodies until he was sitting on the couch and she was straddling his lap, facing him. She put her hands on his shoulders, and he put his on her waist. Then he lifted and lowered her over him, again and again, until finally, finally, he seemed to be deep enough. They both cried out when their orgasms shook them at the same time. Then Pax was spilling himself inside her, and she was claiming him with the heat of her own response.

For one long moment, neither moved, as if they were suspended in time. Then Emma leaned forward and kissed him, becoming aroused all over again in the scent of herself that surrounded him. She wasn't finished with him yet, she realized. She already wanted the next time, which would be so much more thorough. Pax seemed to want that, too, because he gently ended the kiss and removed her from his lap, then stood. Without saying a word, he took her hand and guided her back to his bedroom, turning on the bedside lamp before turning down the bed and going about the removal of what was left of his clothing. Emma wanted to be naked with him, too, wanted to feel every inch of his skin against every inch of hers. So she pushed her skirt over her hips, pulled her shirt over her head and left both neglected on the floor. Then she covered the few steps left between her and Pax.

But she switched off the bedside lamp before joining him in bed so that he wouldn't see the tattoo on her back. If he asked for a reason why she suddenly wanted darkness around them, she'd find some way to be honest with him. But he didn't. He only welcomed her with open arms, moving his body alongside hers again until they were indeed skin to skin, head to toe.

This time when they made love, it truly was lovemaking. He wasn't quite ready to penetrate her again, so they explored each other with their hands and mouths instead until both were finally satisfied. Well, at least as satisfied as they could be for now. Emma didn't think there would ever come a time when she'd had enough of Pax. But she looked forward to enjoying him for what she hoped would be a very long time.

Afterward, in the soft, silent darkness surrounding them, as they snuggled into each other, spent and exhausted, she even heard herself tell him that she loved him, something she'd never said to anyone before. She didn't know what made her say it. It just came out. In that moment, she did love Pax. Maybe she had loved him from day one. Maybe it would only last for tonight. Maybe it would last forever. But she did love him. So she told him that a second time. Then she ducked her head into the curve of his neck and nestled more closely against him.

And just before she drifted into sleep, she heard him say it back to her. But he said *I love you, too, Emma.* She knew it didn't matter that he'd called her by a name that wasn't hers, since that was the name he knew her by. But it did matter. He was falling for a woman she had made up. A woman he didn't know. Even if, in fact, he knew her better than anyone else ever had.

She needed to fix all that. She needed to make clear that even if she wasn't Emma Brown, she was the woman he knew and had come to love. She needed to tell him the truth. And she would.

Just as soon as she had the chance.

Chapter Ten

For the first time in the ten years he had lived in his house, Pax woke up to someone in the bed beside him who wasn't a cat. Without even looking, he hit the Snooze button on the alarm as he always did, remembering that he and Emma would need to be on the road soon. Eyes still closed, he lay on his side facing her, his arm draped over the warm, soft skin of her waist, his palm cupping her breast, her cotton-clad ass pressing into the cradle of his naked thighs, and—

His eyes snapped opened. When they had finally fallen asleep in the wee small hours, they had both been hot and sweaty and naked. Now Emma was not only wearing her panties again, having retrieved them from where he'd tossed them onto the floor in the living room, but she'd slipped her T-shirt back on, too. At some point, she had woken up, risen, and half dressed, then had come back to bed to join him. He'd been sleeping so soundly, he hadn't even stirred.

He remembered her turning off the lamp before they went to bed. It couldn't have been due to her inhibitions, because they'd made wild love in the living room with the lights blazing. And she'd made love here in the bedroom like a woman without an inhibition in the world. The way they'd come together last night—both times—had been some of the hottest, most erotic, most intense sex he'd ever had. The way they'd responded to each other had been nothing short of licentious. Salacious, even. He'd need a whole thesaurus to describe how they'd been together last night. Nothing had been off-limits for either of them. He never would have guessed she would want to put a barrier of clothing between them before morning.

Not that her state of dress did anything to put a damper on his desire for her. On the contrary, just the thought of pulling down her panties now stirred him to life. With one hand still covering her breast, he dipped the other into the scant cotton garment, inching his fingers between her legs to find the feminine heart of her. She moaned sleepily at the contact, opening her legs to allow him better access. Then she covered his hand with hers to guide him more deliberately to where they both wanted him to be. He surged to life against her as she pressed his fingers against her damp flesh, moving his hard member against the soft swell of her bottom and loving the friction created by the fabric covering it. For long moments, he only continued to finger her and rubbed himself into the soft cleft of her rump. Then, when he couldn't help himself any longer, he pulled her panties down just enough to allow him entry into her wet heat from behind. She gasped softly and groaned, reaching behind both of them to grasp his hard buttocks and urge him deeper still. He jerked her panties completely off of her, then turned her until she was on all fours in front of him. Then he grasped her waist with both hands and drove himself inside her, deeper, harder, faster, until they both came again.

But when he took the hem of her T-shirt and started to push it upward to place soft butterfly kisses against her naked back, she pulled away from him, falling into bed on her back again, gasping and panting. For one weird moment, he felt as if he'd done something to make her unhappy. Then she smiled at him and opened her arms wide, and he fell into her embrace. An embrace that was warm and welcoming and loving. Yes, loving. In spite of her brief retreat, she'd made clear that she wanted him again. So he lowered his head between her legs and made sure she enjoyed herself again, too.

When they finally lay side by side once more, gasping for breath and groping for coherent thought, Pax found himself wondering if he would ever get enough of Emma Brown. He'd never responded to a woman the way he'd responded to her. Not just last night, but for the entire six weeks that he'd known her. And she'd responded to him in ways no woman ever had. Certainly sexually, but in other ways, too. She'd been unfazed by all the questionable details of his past. In fact, with some of the things she'd said, she made him feel better about it. And about himself, too. What was it about her that made him feel as if nothing in his life could ever go wrong again?

"You're incredible, you know that?" he told her breathlessly.

She turned her head to look at him and grinned. "You're not so bad yourself."

He expelled a long, contented sigh. "Last night was like nothing I've ever experienced before."

"Same for me."

"When can we do it again?"

She laughed lightly. "Let's just get through this day first, okay?"

The way she said that gave him pause. There was something in her voice that made her sound as if she were anxious about something. He wondered how that was possible after last night. He didn't think he could ever be anxious about anything again. Emma had told him she loved him. And he had replied in kind. It was hard to worry about anything after something like that.

"What time is it?" she asked him.

He looked at the clock. "Time to get up. We need to be on the road in half an hour if we want to get you back to Summerlight by eight."

They shared one more kiss before each moved to their side of the bed and rose. Pax told her she could have the first shower, half hoping she would tell him that that was okay, they could shower together. Instead, she told him thanks and headed for the spare room to retrieve her bag. In minutes, he heard the shower turn on.

Ah, well. Maybe next time.

In spite of the way night had brought them closer in so many ways, she was still a puzzle to him, his Emma. Even so, she was revealing more of herself every time they met. Eventually, he hoped, they would know everything there was to know about each other. In the meantime...

He grinned as he headed to his dresser for fresh

clothes, replaying the highlights of last night—of which there had been many—in his head. Well. In the meantime, he would look forward to uncovering Emma even more.

Pax hit Send on an email to his department head with the finalized versions of his fall syllabi, then headed to his kitchen for a celebratory IPA. The hiss of the beer opening was one of his favorite sounds, because he only heard it when he was rewarding himself for a job well done. Plus, it was Friday, and the week had been more than a little hectic. He hadn't seen Emma in person once since they parted ways in Sudbury the week before. They'd texted and spoken on the phone daily, naturally, and a couple of times they'd FaceTimed, but that was it. He missed her. And he wouldn't be seeing her again for another—he looked at his watch—twelve hours. He was picking her up at Summerlight in the morning, then they were going to drive up to Seneca Falls to spend the day together. She wanted to see the Women's Rights National Historical Park. Pax wanted to see the bridge from *It's a Wonderful Life.* Win-win, as far as he was concerned.

Even better, they'd be spending the night together again afterward, despite having to sleep—and other stuff—in Emma's tiny bed in Emma's tiny room. Tiny spaces didn't matter when you liked being as close as they did. And the fact that they would be able to sleep late this time because it would be a Sunday off for both of them—and then spend a second long, leisurely day together in Sudbury—was just a bonus.

But seeing Emma again was still an unbearable night away. He started to text her, then realized he'd already bugged her that way three times today and really didn't have any reason to now, other than to tell her he missed her. Which he'd already told her three times. They'd also confirmed and reconfirmed their plans for tomorrow, so there was no reason to go over those again. He could tell her he'd finished with his pre-term prep for classes and share that celebration with her. But that was kind of a lame thing to celebrate with someone else, and he really didn't want to spend any more time thinking about it than he had to.

He just wanted to see Emma in person—that was all. He missed her. A lot. He just wished the two of them could wake up beside each other every morning, the way they had here at his place the week before. Hell, he wouldn't even mind waking up next to her every morning in her tiny bed in her tiny room at the inn, cramped though that would be. It would just bring them closer. Literally and figuratively.

He made his way out to his living room, gave Cairo a few scritches behind the ear, then started to sit down on the sofa beside him. But he stopped and turned instead, then strode over to the doors that led to his patio and opened them. Outside, Cayuga Heights was quiet on this Friday night. Although his next-door neighbors seemed to be entertaining on the other side of the privacy fence, they were doing it politely. The jazz was muted, and the conversation was muffled. Whatever was on the grill smelled amazing. Glasses clinked, people laughed, and someone raised their voice enough to praise Ornette Coleman as the greatest saxophonist of all time, only to be challenged that no, it was 'trane or Bird or Getz.

Pax couldn't help but smile. His house here in the heart of academia was so different from Emma's quiet little room at Summerlight. But even with what passed for "noise" in his neighborhood, he loved it here. He still couldn't believe this was his life now, a life so different from the one he might have had to endure otherwise. He couldn't imagine where he'd be now if he was still traveling with his family. Hell, he could have been in prison by now, for all he knew. And he sure as hell never would have met Emma.

Whom he still missed.

He strode out onto the patio, into the warm summer night, made two laps around the backyard, then went inside again. He was restless. And he missed Emma. Had he mentioned he was missing Emma? 'Cause he for sure was. He sat down on the sofa next to Cairo and picked up the Patricia Highsmith book he'd started earlier in the week. Fifteen minutes later, he realized he had no idea what he'd read and put it back down again. Cairo looked at him as if to say *Dude, relax—you'll see her soon*, but Pax was still restless. He pulled up *LA Noire* on PlayStation, played for even fewer than fifteen minutes, then switched it off. He'd been streaming and loving *Altered Carbon* and was halfway through it, but he doubted he'd get more than fifteen minutes into that, either, before becoming distracted again.

He opened his MacBook. Maybe he could work on some of the promo for Summerlight and get his Emma fix vicariously. He went to the web page he maintained for the inn to see if anything needed updating, but everything looked good. So he opened the folder with all the video and photos Haven had shot and sent to him to see if anything there might be useful. A half dozen pictures in was one that included Emma, a candid shot of her from behind, dusting the very bookcases she'd been tending in Haven's office the day he first met her. He smiled at both the image and the memory of that day. He was about to click through to the next photo when he noticed something on her back. She was reaching up with a feather duster in the photo, enough so that the T-shirt she was wearing had dipped beneath the nape of her neck.

He enlarged the photo. It looked as if the top part of a tattoo was peeking out from beneath the collar of her shirt. Huh. He'd had no idea she had a tattoo. Of course, he'd never seen her bare back, either. Oh well. He grinned. Hopefully he'd see it this weekend. More than once.

He did actually manage to get a little work done for the inn, but his concentration there, too, eventually waned. He still missed Emma. Still wanted to be with her.

Oh, what the hell. If he couldn't see her in person, he'd spend some time with her virtually. Pulling up Google on his laptop, he entered the name *Emma Brown*... only to have more than a hundred million hits come up. Damn. He put the name in quotes. Oh, great. Only six and a half million now. He clicked on the Verbatim option. Nope. Still way too much to wade through. There was an Emma Brown high school track star in Lubbock, Texas; an Emma Brown hamster care specialist on YouTube; an Emma Brown, celebrity chef—at least she was a celebrity on Tenerife, in the Canary Islands; an Emma Brown, Tasmanian zookeeper; an Emma Brown, cheesemaker...

Yeah, this was getting him nowhere. Fine. *Emma Brown* in quotation marks followed by *Altoona, PA*. Wow. There was even more than one Emma Brown just in Altoona. But it didn't take long for Pax to find the one he was looking for. He knew it was his Emma because there was so little information about her. She'd told him how she'd never been a big user of social media because her parents hadn't been able to afford internet access when she was a kid, so she'd always had to resort to the computers at school or in the public library. And how, even now, she just didn't feel the need, so she'd never opened accounts on Facebook or Instagram or whatever. He respected that, even if he wasn't quite sure how she did it. If he couldn't go online daily, he would have felt like a part of him was missing.

He scrolled through the few mentions of her that he could find. A piece in the *Altoona Mirror* from more than a decade ago in an article about hospital volunteers, something he remembered her telling him she'd been once upon a time. Then another article in which she was quoted as a participant in a Walk to End Alzheimer's— *It's a [expletive deleted] awful [expletive deleted] disease that needs a [expletive deleted] cure right this [expletive deleted] instant.*

He grinned. Wow, she'd really cleaned up her language since then… He checked the date on the article. Huh. Only three years ago. She'd talked as though she'd been gone from Altoona long before then. Maybe she'd gone back home for some special occasion. He did some more scrolling and found another mention of her, in an obituary for her great-grandmother, where she was listed as a surviving family member. But no mention of any parents being surviving family members, too, even though she'd said they were still around. Maybe they'd gone no-contact.

As much as he'd hoped reading about Emma would make him feel closer to her again, for some reason, Pax was only feeling kind of unsettled. He tried to put it down to his restlessness earlier at not seeing her for so long. But there was something creeping around at the edges of his brain that just felt a little…off.

He clicked on Images. And there she was. Fuzzy and from a distance, but at least there was something. He started to relax again as he tapped on the first photo, one on the page of the hospital where she'd volunteered along with a bunch of other volunteers. Emma was in the back row, sandwiched between a woman with a big beehive hairdo and a man wearing a clerical collar. Pax opened the image in a new tab and enlarged it, something that brought Emma closer but weakened the quality of the photo. She'd told him she did the volunteer thing when she was in high school. She didn't seem to have changed much at all since then. And speaking of high school, he found another photo of her that was from the Crestwood High School yearbook the year she'd been in the homecoming court. It was on the Facebook page of a classmate—again posted more than a decade ago—who he quickly discovered had been the homecoming princess that year. The quality on this picture was surprisingly better than the one from the hospital site, and when Pax enlarged it, it was much easier to make out Emma's face. The minute he did, though, he frowned. There was something about it that looked...strange.

When he enlarged this photo, he saw that it had been photoshopped. Not that that was a big deal, since high schools must certainly have had access to Photoshop for at least a decade and had probably been teaching kids how to use it, so they would naturally shop some of the pictures in their yearbook. But whoever had shopped this one had done a shockingly good job. Better than a high school student learning about Photoshop would do. Better enough that, to any casual observer, the photograph didn't look altered at all. But Pax wasn't a casual observer of Photoshop. He was a pro who used it all the time.

He went back to the photo of Emma with the other the hospital volunteers and studied that one more closely. It wasn't as obvious, but that one had been shopped, too. He went back to the search results and pulled up the few other photos there were of her. One from a friend's social media that hadn't been updated for nearly five years—a selfie with the two of them sitting on the edge of a fountain in downtown Altoona. Yep. Shopped. And Pax was pretty sure the face of Emma on this one was from a shot taken at the same time as one of the others. The pose was different, but the hairstyle was exactly the same, even though the two shots had supposedly been taken years apart.

Digging deeper, he found an entire yearbook for Crestwood High School of Altoona, Pennsylvania, on one of those websites that hosted them and scrolled through them until he found one that corresponded to what would have been Emma's sophomore year. He located her among her classmates easily, but he frowned when he realized that it, too, had been shopped. He scrolled through the whole yearbook until he found another picture that identified her by name. It was of a female student sitting at the back of a sparsely populated classroom. But where everyone else was rapt with whatever the teacher in front of them was saying, Emma was looking out the window. The caption beneath the photo read, *Looks like Emma Brown would rather be anywhere but Mrs. Holstein's Algebra II class.* Her head was turned almost all the way away from the camera, but not entirely. Pax looked at the photo very, very closely. This one, he realized, had *not* been photoshopped. But nor, he was reasonably certain, was it Emma Brown in the photo. Not his Emma Brown anyway. He didn't care what the caption said.

His stomach pitched when he realized what he was looking at. Someone had altered nearly every photo of Emma Brown from Altoona, Pennsylvania, that existed on the web, regardless of where that photo was published. Putting aside, for a moment, the fact that that had even happened, he marveled at how very good at all things internet someone would have to be to do that. Whoever had done it had had to hack into no fewer than five different websites, one of which was a national corporate hospital. Only a major hacker could do that. And then to digitally alter the photos required another skill set altogether. To do it all without bringing attention to oneself was yet another show of just how good at what they were doing this person had been. Pax could count on two hands how many people he knew of who could do something like this.

And Emma Brown of Altoona, Pennsylvania, wasn't one of them.

Why had someone photoshopped Emma Brown's image in all those different shots? *Who* had photoshopped Emma Brown's image? The answer to the second question was obvious. Emma must have done it herself. But was it the Emma Brown he knew from Summerlight or the actual Emma Brown from Altoona? And if it was the actual Emma Brown from Altoona, what was her connection to the Emma Brown from Summerlight? Why would she have photoshopped someone else's face—why would she have photoshopped Emma Brown of Summerlight's face—over her own?

Unless it wasn't the Emma Brown from Altoona who had done that. Which meant it must have been Emma Brown from Summerlight. *His* Emma Brown. But again, why? Why would she paste her face over the face of someone who didn't even have much of an internet presence? What point was there in taking someone no one had ever heard of or cared about and replacing her face with a different someone that no one had ever heard of or cared about? That didn't make any sense.

Just who the hell was Emma Brown? Not the one from Altoona, who'd obviously hated Algebra II, but the one living on the top floor of Summerlight in Sudbury, New York, whom Pax had fallen in lo—

He stopped the thought before it could fully form. His brain was buzzing with too many other thoughts at the moment. And the more he thought, the more confused he became. And the more confused he became, the angrier he started to feel. Little by little, things began to fall into place for Pax. Those Emma jigsaw puzzle pieces he'd thought he'd lost on the floor suddenly found their way back onto the table and into the picture. All those things about her that had seemed to be at odds with who he knew her to be, all the strange things she'd said that she'd hastily tried to excuse or cover afterward…all of it came back to haunt him.

That time she told him this part of the country was so different from anyplace else she'd seen—including the area where she'd allegedly grown up. The zippered hot-pink miniskirt she'd loved at the thrift store that had been the complete antithesis of the flowy, flowered one she had on. Her savviness about so many things tech when she'd assured him she was in no way techy. Her weird adamance that he promise to never photograph or film her. He replayed every moment they'd spent together and identified even more things that he hadn't much noticed before but gave him pause now.

There had been signs all along, a lot of them, that Emma Brown wasn't who she seemed—who she claimed—to be, but Pax had been too besotted to catch them. He'd been so busy being awed by how genuine

and real and honest she'd seemed to be—hah—that he
hadn't noticed the obvious lies right in front of his face.
Damn, he really had been away from the family for a
long time if he couldn't even read a person that obvious anymore. Just who was—what was—the woman
he'd fallen in love with?

His head was spinning. What the hell was going on?
Why had Emma lied to him? Because no matter what
was going on, it was clear Emma *had* lied to him. A
lot. For one thing, she wasn't Emma Brown from Altoona. He was gonna go out on a limb and say she wasn't
Emma Brown from anywhere else, either. So who was
she?

His stomach pitched again. If she'd lied to him about
her name and her past and where she was from, it was
a safe bet she'd lied about a lot of other things, too. For
all he knew, she'd lied about everything she'd ever told
him. Where was she from? He had no idea. Had she
actually worked any of the jobs she told him she'd held
over the years? No clue. Had she visited all the places
she said she had? Got him. Did she really like all the
books and movies she'd professed to love? Who knew?
Or had all of it been a carefully crafted lie to—

To what? he asked himself again. Why would anyone
pretend to be someone they weren't unless they were
looking to take advantage of the person they were lying
to? Or unless there was something about them that was
so heinous they couldn't risk anyone else finding out
about it? What was Emma's—or whoever the hell she
was—secret that she didn't want anyone to know? Not
even someone she'd come to love like Pax?

But then, had that been a lie, too? Did she really love him? Did she even like him? Or had she just been feeding him lines because he was nothing more than a means to some kind of end he couldn't imagine yet?

Just who the hell was the woman living at Summerlight that he'd spent the last month and a half falling in love with? And why, dammit, had she lied to him, even after knowing how much he detested liars? Not just once, but a million times? Anyone who could do that couldn't possibly care about him at all.

He tried to tell himself he was overreacting, that there had to be some good reason for why she was pretending to be someone else. He tried to tell himself that even if she was pretending to be someone else, some of what she had said over the past several weeks must have been true. He tried to tell himself that even if she'd lied about other things, her feelings for him were real.

He tried. But he didn't quite believe himself.

How had this happened? Having grown up around liars and con artists, he'd developed an uncanny ability to know when other people were misrepresenting themselves. Usually within minutes of meeting someone, he knew whether or not they were being honest or even just disingenuous. He could read people. He knew people. His livelihood had depended on that for more than half his life. But with Emma...

Emma had blindsided him. Not for an instant had he felt like she was misrepresenting anything about herself. Yeah, she'd been wary and cautious around him at first. But he'd just figured that was because she was wary and cautious by nature. Never in a gazillion years would he have thought she was being that way because she was sizing him up as a mark—the same way he had done with so many people himself when he was a kid.

She'd played him. But good. Not that he probably didn't deserve it after some of the things he'd done to other people when he was young. But damn. He never saw it coming. She was even better at duplicity than he'd been.

He had no idea what to do now. He would still go to Summerlight in the morning as planned, but he was reasonably certain there would be no day trip to Seneca Falls tomorrow. One thing was sure, though. By day's end, he *would* know who Emma Brown of Sudbury, New York, really was. And he *would* know why she had lied to him. After that…

Well now. That just depended on what Emma said. And how she said it. And whether or not she was finally telling him the truth.

Chapter Eleven

The second Emma saw Pax Saturday morning, she knew there was something wrong. Really wrong. Like to the point that, somehow, she even knew they wouldn't be spending the day together. Not having fun in Seneca Falls anyway.

Last night, she'd gone to bed knowing this would be the day she told him the truth. After the day and night they'd spent together last week, she couldn't go on being dishonest with him. Not that she'd really been dishonest, since, after replaying everything she'd said to him in her head all week, she'd realized she really hadn't lied to him about anything other than her name. But she hadn't been honest with him, either—not completely. She'd awoken in his bed last weekend wanting to tell him everything then. How could she not want to tell him everything after all they had shared the night before? They'd shared themselves completely that night, in body, in spirit, in soul, in…love. She naturally wanted to share the rest of herself with him, too, after that. All of herself.

But they'd had to hurry around his place to get back to Sudbury on time that day. Then they'd both had work to do at Summerlight. Lunch in town at Dragonfly Café had been nice, but it had been too public a venue for everything she had to tell him. Then there had been more work at Summerlight, and then Pax had had to go home.

Today, she had decided, would be ideal. They'd be alone together, with plenty of time to talk. All week, she had framed and reframed what she wanted to say to him and how she wanted to say it, until she'd come to a point where she knew she could make him understand why she hadn't been honest with him from the start.

She'd figured he might be a little stung at first that she hadn't trusted him before now. But she'd known it would only be at first, and she'd known it would only be temporary. Pax was a good guy. Once he realized what had been at stake for her, once he knew how she had had to live for the past near year because of it, once he comprehended how very terrified she'd been by all that had happened to her—by all that still could happen to her—he would understand why she hadn't been able to tell him everything to begin with. She'd been so sure of that.

Until she saw him standing at the foot of the stairs in Summerlight's lobby, glaring at her as if she were evil incarnate. Until the very air around him felt icy and noxious and scary.

What had happened between yesterday and today that would bring about such a change? Yesterday his texts had been full of humor and affection. The whole past week had been filled with such texts. Plus phone calls and FaceTimes that had had both of them laughing and cooing and making plans. Plans beyond just today's trip to Seneca Falls, too. They'd talked about how they would manage seeing each other once the new semester started for him and after Summerlight opened for her. They had talked about things happening in their future—*their* future—that were months away. Emma had never planned that far ahead for anything with another person. But with Pax, it had felt totally normal to make plans for a future that went beyond a few days or weeks ahead. Looking at him now...

Her breath hitched in her chest as she gazed down at him from the top step on the second floor, where she'd halted the instant she saw him. Looking at him now, she feared they wouldn't have a future beyond the next few minutes.

Her gaze never left his as she picked her way down the rest of the stairs. She'd actually gone into town this week to buy something new to wear for today's outing, since Pax had already seen her in every stitch of clothing she owned and she'd wanted to wear something special for what had been feeling like a bold step forward in their relationship. The sleeveless summer sheath fell to nearly her ankles in a flow of pale yellow linen, buttoning from hem to scooped neckline with pearly flower-shaped buttons. It was so unlike anything she would have bought as Amber Finch, but Emma had fallen in love with it the minute she laid eyes on it. Her heart had raced at the image of Pax unbuttoning each of those buttons, one by one, at day's end, when they returned to Summerlight to spend the night together. By the time her feet hit the foyer floor, however, she knew there would be no unbuttoning tonight. Judging by his expression, she began to worry there might never be any unbuttoning again.

What had happened since yesterday to make him so angry?

In spite of the differences in their height—Pax stood nearly a foot taller than she—Emma had never felt like he towered over her. He'd always been so accessible, so sweet and gentle, that his height had never felt threatening at all. Today it did. He didn't just tower over her, he loomed. All of him felt threatening in that moment. Instinctively, she stopped where she was and stayed frozen at the foot of the staircase with a good ten feet still separating them. Deep down inside, the part of her that had been constantly poised for flight since fleeing Seattle—a part that had lain dormant since coming to Sudbury—lurched into escape mode again. For the first time since taking up residence at Summerlight, Emma was ready to bolt. She was ready to do whatever she had to do to keep herself safe from harm. And in that moment, the harm she felt like she had to keep herself safe from was Pax.

She told herself he wouldn't harm her. Not the way virtually every other man she'd encountered since last September had tried to harm her. Pax wasn't like those guys at all. His masculinity was in no way toxic. On the contrary, he was one of the purest, most authentic people she'd ever met. Even if, at the moment, there was something about him that wasn't exactly...*non*toxic.

"We need to talk," he said without preamble, his voice edged with something that bordered on, well, toxic.

In spite of his obvious belligerence, Emma made

herself smile. And she injected as much lightness into her voice as she could when she replied, "Well, hello to you, too."

He only glared at her harder. "Where can we talk?"

In spite of the turmoil tearing her up inside, she said, "Haven and Bennett are out for the day. There's no one home but you and me. We can talk right here."

She started to ask him what was wrong, then realized she didn't want to know. Not that she could avoid finding out, since he was obviously determined to *talk*—or something—about whatever it was. But she couldn't see any reason to rush things.

He looked around the cavernous foyer and shook his head in reply to her proposal. She hoped it wasn't because he was planning to raise his voice and feared all the shouting might bring down the whole house.

"Haven's office, then," he told her.

Before she could agree or make another suggestion, he spun around and started making his way in that direction, leaving Emma to catch up. Not once did he slow his stride. Not once did he say a word over his shoulder. Not once did he look back at her.

Whatever was wrong, it was massive. For the life of her, she couldn't imagine what had happened in a matter of hours to make him respond to her this way. There was no way he could know who she was. None. She was reasonably sure there was no way he could have discovered she was lying to him, either. But every muscle in her body was tensing up, and every survival instinct she had was careening into overdrive. She was beginning to feel the same way she'd felt in Seattle when those first three goons had broken down her front door as she was escaping through the back. Red alerts were going on all around her, telling her to watch her back. To run away. To escape the threat.

But Pax wasn't a threat, she told herself again. There was no need to run. No need to watch her back.

Not that her body or brain listened to her reassurances. With every step she took, her feeling of dread compounded. By the time she caught up to him in Haven's office that dread was threatening to overtake her. He was standing at the center of the room, legs splayed, hands on hips, in a posture that could only be called aggressive. For the first time, she noticed that he wasn't dressed in any of his usual whimsical attire. Today he was wearing blue jeans and a plain black T-shirt.

Battle gear, she couldn't help thinking. Because he was clearly ready to go on the attack.

"Just who the hell are you?" he demanded when she came through the office door.

She stopped immediately, staying framed in the exit to give her quick access to a way out—and far enough from him to get a good head start should she indeed need to flee. The realization that she had positioned herself that way so instinctively didn't sit well with her.

Her stomach dropped at the question, and she felt vaguely sick. He knew she'd been lying. Despite her reassurances to herself, somehow, he had figured out her ruse.

Even realizing that, she tried to sound innocent when she replied, "What do you mean, who am I? I'm Emma Brown."

Liar, she thought. She wasn't Emma Brown. She was lying to Pax again. No matter how much she had told herself over the past two months that she wasn't lying to him, she had been lying to him. And now, somehow, he knew that.

Although she wouldn't have thought it was possible, his expression went even harder. "No, you're not. I don't know who you are, but you're not Emma Brown. You weren't born in Altoona. You didn't graduate from Crestwood High School. You weren't in the homecoming court. And you sure as hell never won a red ribbon at the county fair. You're not Emma Brown. So who are you?"

Instead of answering his question, since the more he said, the more menacing he seemed, Emma only replied, "How did you find out?"

He shook his head. "You still can't be honest, can you? Answer the question."

She said nothing in response to that. No sense lying any more than she already had.

Pax did reply, though. He told her about how he had been missing her the night before—missing *her*, a liar—so he googled her. And how he realized pretty quickly that the photos of her he found on the web— "Excuse me, the photos I found of the *real* Emma Brown of Altoona"—had been photoshopped with her likeness in place of the original subject. And how everything she'd told him about being Emma Brown— and hell, Altoona, for that matter—were just facts and figures that aligned with public information about both. He told her how he'd tried to do a reverse image search for the faked face on those photos but had come up empty somehow. Meaning whoever she *really* was had been wiped clean from the web, and it took a pretty major tech pro to do that.

Although it was true that Emma was a pretty major tech pro, there was no way she could have wiped herself from the Net after what happened with Travis Swope, because there was just too much about her on the web to wipe clean, and new stuff was being posted every day. The reason he hadn't been able to find her through a reverse image search was because all the photos of her on the web prior to the Swope debacle had been of her in full makeup, which the algorithms couldn't gibe with the handful of photos Emma had taken of herself clean faced after leaving Seattle to photoshop over the real Emma Brown. And any photos of her clean faced in Seattle uploaded by Swope's minions had been of her in profile looking away or with her hand in front of her face.

There were no earlier online images of her without makeup because she hadn't had social media when she was a kid. Her parents hadn't been able to afford internet access, and the school computers had prohibited students from uploading images of themselves for the sake of internet safety. It had been years after leaving home that Emma had even used social media, and by then, she'd been a cosmetics diva. She *wished* she could have erased herself from the internet. Since she couldn't, she'd simply uploaded a version no one else would be able to recognize. Including the bots whose job it was to identify people and things through reverse image searches.

"So I repeat," Pax said now, "who the hell are you?"

Emma inhaled a deep breath and reminded herself that today was the day she had planned to tell him the truth anyway, so to just spill it. But she hadn't planned on revealing herself to this Pax. This angry, combative and, yes, scary Pax. This Pax who suddenly seemed *a lot* like the guys who had been terrorizing her for almost a year.

This version of him was a stranger. She never would have suspected he had such a menacing side to him. Even if she was the one responsible for his current state of anger, she couldn't tell the truth to this Pax. This Pax had clearly already decided she was an awful person— she was a liar. And a liar was someone for whom he had no sympathy. No compassion. And, judging by the look of him at the moment, no mercy. There was no way she could confess the truth to him right now. Not when she didn't trust what his reaction might be.

But she could at least confess to the big one. "You're right," she said softly. "My name isn't Emma Brown, and I'm not from Altoona."

He nodded curtly. "Tell me something I don't know. Like who you really are."

She couldn't tell him that last one. Not yet. Not until his anger cooled and he could be more open to understanding. But she could tell him a few things he didn't know that would be truthful.

"I grew up in the western part of the country," she told him. "I'm twenty-nine years old and a Scorpio.

I'm also a terrible baker, I'm in no way comfortable in hospitals, I never even went to a homecoming dance, let alone been a member of the court. I never went to Dickinson or any other college. But everything else I told you about me, Pax…" She sighed shakily. "That's all true. I never lied to you about any of those things."

His mouth flattened into a tight line. He didn't believe her. Not that she was really surprised. But she would have liked to think the two of them had gotten close enough that he would at least give her the benefit of the doubt. That he would at least give her a chance.

"Why did you lie to me?" he asked.

She shook her head miserably. "I can't tell you that." She started to add *Not yet*, but at the moment, she honestly wasn't sure if she would ever be able to tell him the truth, and she'd lied enough.

"Why can't you tell me?" he demanded.

"I can't tell you that, either. I'm sorry," she hurried on. "I wish I could, but I can't. Not with you being like this."

"Like what? Feeling totally betrayed because a woman I thought I loved is suddenly a woman I don't even know?"

His use of the past tense of love made her wince. Not that she was surprised by that, either. He was hurting. She got that. But that was another reason she couldn't be honest with him now. People who were hurt lashed out. Sometimes they lashed out in ways they regretted later. She didn't think Pax would turn her in once he found out who she was. He wouldn't retaliate that cruelly. But in the heat of the moment, he could reveal in the wrong venue online that, *Hey, everybody, the new housekeeper of Summerlight Bed and Breakfast in Sudbury, New York, is none other than Amber Finch—isn't that wild?* and her life would turn to an even newer, even fresher, living hell. Probably, he wouldn't do that.

But he might. She just didn't know for sure.

"I understand why you might think you don't know me," she told him, "but it isn't true, Pax. You know me better than anyone."

At this, he looked like he wanted to throw something. Hard. He opened his mouth again, but she quickly continued to cut him off.

"And I haven't betrayed you," she assured him. "I am exactly the woman you think I am. I'm just not named Emma Brown. Everything the two of us have experienced together, it's all been honest and true."

He actually laughed out loud at that. "Honest, right. True. I've spent the last two months caring for a woman who now admits she's not the woman she said she was."

At this, Emma bit back a growl of frustration. "No, as I just told you, I am exactly the woman you've come to know and...and care about for the last two months. It's only my name that's a pretense."

He nodded roughly at this. "Then you won't mind telling me what you were doing for a living before you came to Sudbury, right? Or where you lived? Or what brought you to Sudbury in the first place? Because all of those are a big part of the woman you are. It's not just your name that's missing from this...this...this whatever it was we had going."

Was. He was using the past tense again.

"So tell me, whoever you are, about all those aspects of your life."

She closed her eyes, feeling defeated. "I can't tell you those things," she said.

"So I really don't know who you are."

She expelled a sound that was at once bereft and sardonic. "Pax, you know me better than anyone in my entire life ever has."

He muttered a sound of disgust. "Never say anything like that to me again. Don't lie."

She was losing him. Fast. Even if she couldn't tell him the whole truth now, she had to tell him something, something honest, which might at least give him pause. She hadn't said a word to anyone since leaving Seattle about being on the run and in hiding. The few times any conversation had turned to the idle *So what's your story?* type stuff, she'd either brushed off the other person's interest or she'd lied through her teeth when she replied. She couldn't lie to Pax anymore. But she couldn't brush it off with him, either. With him in the mood he was in, she couldn't tell him everything. But she had to tell him something. Maybe if she just told him the essence of the problem without going into detail or exposing herself as Amber Finch, bounty-hunted nemesis of the manosphere, he would be more understanding.

"Okay, I'll tell you the truth," she said wearily.

"Finally."

The word dripped with disdain. She hoped she wasn't making a mistake by opening up even a little.

"So for the last several months," she began, "I've kind of had to be…in hiding."

She waited to see how he would respond to that. His response was to not respond at all. He only gazed at her blandly. "You've been in hiding," he echoed. Also blandly.

She nodded.

"And why is that?"

She met his gaze levelly. "Because I've been having to keep a low profile from someone."

He continued to gaze at her as if she were a boring, blank wall. "And what someone is that?"

"Someone who…" Her gaze skittered off of his to fall on a bird that had landed on the windowsill on the other side of the room. She was thankful for the distraction so she wouldn't have to see his reaction when she finished her sentence.

"Someone who wants to…hurt me," she said as evenly as she could even though, inside, she was growing terrified all over again. "Or see me hurt by others. Either way, I haven't been safe for a while, and I'm not sure when I'll be safe again."

When she looked back at Pax, it was to see that he had indeed reacted this time to what she said. His eyes had grown darker, his mouth had flattened into a thin line and his whole expression had gone hard.

"Like an ex-boyfriend?" he asked. His voice was edged with something vaguely frightening when he added, "An *abusive* ex-boyfriend?"

She shook her head. "We were never involved." Then because that wasn't quite true, since she and Travis

Swope had indeed been involved, at least online, for all of ten minutes, she said, "Not like that anyway."

"But it's a guy, right?"

She nodded. Then she clarified, "More than one, really. He...knows a lot of people, and he got them involved in his mission to make my life a living hell. But yeah. One guy in particular set the wheels in motion. And I'm not going to be safe until the wheels stop turning. And they won't stop turning until he finds me or changes his mind. And he's not the kind of guy to change his mind—trust me."

She winced at her own wording. Pax didn't seem to care much for her phrasing, either. But his expression cleared some, and he studied her in silence while he digested what she'd said.

Finally he asked, "Why does this guy want to hurt you?"

This was the part where it was going to sound like she was being overly dramatic. Or, worse, lying. But she wasn't lying. And it was hard to dismiss as drama death threats, rape threats, being chased, and physical attacks on one's person.

Even so, she steeled herself for his response when she told him the truth. "Because I made him look bad in front of his...friends."

Not that Travis Swope considered any of his minions friends. They were just a bunch of patsies he could squeeze money and internet fame from to make himself feel important. But he always called them his friends, and they always found some kind of weird validation

224 KEEPING HER SECRET

in that. Enough to throw money at his dubious manly teachings and do whatever he bade them do.

Pax's expression changed again, and she could tell she was losing him once more with her admission. He didn't believe her. He was more convinced than ever now that she was lying.

"You expect me to believe that you had change your name and go on the run—*go into hiding*—because you made some guy look bad in front of his friends?"

She knew it sounded lame the way she'd worded it. Miserably, she added, "It was a lot of friends. And I made him look really, *really* bad. And he's the kind of person who thinks his image is everything."

Pax nodded, then expelled a sound that punctuated just how very, very, *very* full of crap he thought she was. "Right. So you insulted this guy, and he was so offended, you had to disappear." Then he said "Right" again, to reiterate just how much he didn't believe a word she was saying.

Okay, so trying to explain—trying to tell the truth—had just convinced him even more certainly that she was lying. Why had she thought it would be a good idea to come clean in the first place?

"It's complicated," she concluded lamely, relying on his own description of his early-life situation. Maybe that would at least make him a little less dubious.

But he only responded to her the way she had responded to him then. "Sounds like."

But where she hadn't been dismissive of his own experiences when she said it, he was clearly being dismissive of hers. Not that she really blamed him. Without the full story—which he had at least given her with his accounts—she did sound like she was, well, lying.

"I know it sounds like a bad movie," she admitted. "But he's a scary guy with a lot of money and power and influence. The kind of guy who definitely has the ability to make a person's life miserable. If he knew where I was now, he would come after me or he would send his flying monkeys after me, and he and they would make things very unpleasant for me."

Unpleasant. Right. More like terrifying. And traumatizing. And if some of those guys got their way, potentially fatal. Nothing like having an army of sociopaths at your beck and call. She wished she could deride them as all talk. But the times early on when she had been recognized, the guys who approached her had, you know, *approached* her. They'd put hands on her. Hands that she'd barely been able to escape. And that time a group of them had tried to assault her and been narrowly repelled by a couple who just happened to be passing by…

Emma still got sick to her stomach at the memory. She could imagine, too well, what would have happened to her that day if she hadn't been rescued. What could still happen on any given day if she was recognized again. Even if ninety-nine-point-nine percent of Travis Swope's followers were blowhards, that still left point-one percent who weren't. Point-one percent who could—and would—do her serious harm. And point-one percent of millions was…

Well. Thousands too many.

Pax, however, knew none of that. And in his current

state, she couldn't tell him. At this point, even if she admitted to being Amber Finch, he probably wouldn't believe her. Not until she showed him the tattoo on her back that marked her.

Talk about a rock and a hard place. On one hand, Pax didn't believe her, and she was close to losing him forever. On the other hand, she could tell him the truth and genuinely endanger herself. And even if she told him the truth about herself, there was no guarantee that she wouldn't still lose him. For all she knew, even if he didn't turn her in, he might loathe Amber Finch as much as a million other guys on the web.

One thing did become clear pretty quick, though. He definitely loathed her as phony Emma Brown. "Wow, I didn't think you could lie any worse than you already had," he told her scornfully, "but somehow you have."

"I'm not ly—"

"Don't," he interjected. "Don't ever say a word to me again, about anything. I just want to forget I ever met you."

Her entire body went slack. He couldn't possibly mean that. "Pax, no," she said miserably. "Don't say that."

He expelled a sound of complete disdain. "Why not? It's the truth. Which is more than you've ever said."

Was he really going to be like this? Was he honestly going to give up on them so quickly and with so little attempt at understanding? Could he not give them a little time so that they could both gather their thoughts and work out their feelings and try again to figure things out when their tempers weren't running so high? If he was so willing to think she was so awful so quickly, was he really the guy she'd fallen in love with in the first place?

"I can't talk to you when you're being like this," she said.

"What? Demanding the truth? I know you can't. Because you can't tell the truth. That's the problem."

"I can tell the truth," she told him adamantly, confidently. "You're just not ready to hear it."

At this, his anger only compounded. But he said nothing. Then again, what else was there for him to say? He'd said more than enough already.

As if realizing that, he dropped his hands from his hips and strode forward, toward Emma. She immediately recoiled, leaping backward into the hallway, taking several quick steps in retreat. Her unconscious reaction was enough to tell her she'd been right not to reveal the truth to him. There was a part of her—and it wasn't a small part—that clearly did not trust him. Not the Pax he was being today.

He hesitated at her reaction to his forward motion, stopping just inside the office doorway. Emma inched a few more steps backward, giving him a wide berth to head for the exit. When he realized how she had reacted—in fear, of him—his expression eased a bit. He regrouped quickly, however, holding fast to his anger, as if he'd reminded himself how much she had hurt him.

Emma knew she had hurt him, and for that, she was sorry. But she had never meant to hurt him. Certainly not the way he was deliberately hurting her now.

He spared her one last long look, this one a little less angry than the others he'd thrown at her today and a bit more distressed. As if his fury was waning, to be replaced by the anguish that came with betrayal. Not that Emma had betrayed him. Not that he understood that.

He turned his back on her and made his way down the hall to the front door, never slowing, never missing a step, never looking back. Emma envied him. She knew she would be looking back on this moment for a long, long time. And she knew she would be stumbling a lot.

Pax slammed the front door loudly enough that it seemed to reverberate throughout the entire house. It certainly reverberated throughout Emma. She told herself they would work it out. Somehow. She still planned to tell him the truth—once he cooled off. If she couldn't do it in person, then she'd tell him over the phone. If he didn't answer, she'd send him a long text. If he blocked her... Well. She'd just park herself on his front porch until he would listen to reason.

He would cool off. Eventually. He would listen to reason. Eventually. And he would understand. Eventually. He had to.

He had to.

Chapter Twelve

He wasn't going to listen to reason, Emma discovered two weeks after Pax stormed out of Summerlight never to return. And he never cooled off. No way was he ever going to understand. For two weeks, she'd tried texting him, calling him and emailing him, hoping he would reply in a way that let her know he had calmed down and gone back to being the Pax she knew and loved, the one she could speak to frankly and trust that he would understand. But he'd never replied. Eventually, he'd even blocked her, the ultimate signal that they were through, that he wanted no part of her—ever again. She was *this close* to asking Haven for two weeks off to spend in Ithaca, where she could camp out on his front porch until he had no choice but to talk to her.

Ultimately, she didn't have to do that. Because Pax finally showed up on her front porch instead. Well, okay, not her front porch. Summerlight's front porch. And he didn't come to see her. He came to see, presumably, Haven or Bennett or both—because he for sure didn't come looking for her. Emma watched from where she was working on the side of the house, deadheading shrubs and pruning hedges, but the one time he looked her way, he immediately turned his attention back to the front door and kept moving toward it. She didn't care. She *would* talk to him before he left. Even if she had to go let the air out of one of his tires to do that. Maybe he'd decided things between them were over, but she wasn't ready to call it quits. In spite of the way they had parted the last time they were together, she still loved him. And, she suspected, he still had feelings for her. Strong feelings, too, considering how badly he felt she had betrayed him.

And okay, yes, some of his strong feelings for her were probably not great. There still must be something inside him, somewhere, that still cared for her in a good way. That cared for *them* as a couple and didn't want to throw that away. She had to believe that. What the two of them had found together and shared together wasn't something that could just go away. She loved him. He loved her. Or at least, he had, not so long ago. Love like that didn't just go away. Maybe things between the two of them were bad at the moment, but that didn't mean all was lost. They could work through it. That was what people who were in love did. When something broke, they did whatever they could to fix it. Emma would do whatever she could to fix what was wrong between her and Pax.

Before he left Summerlight today, he would know she was Amber Finch. She would tell him, in great detail, exactly what her life had been like for the past year. She would make him understand why she had had to keep her identity a secret. And if he still wanted no part of her—if, even worse, he outed her to the rest of the world, she would pack her bags and leave Sudbury and go into hiding again. She certainly wouldn't be any worse off doing that than she would be if she stayed here and continued to lie. Either way, she would be losing Pax. Either way, she would be miserable. But at least he would know the truth. And if their relationship ended as a result, that would be on him, not her. She would have done everything she could to mend the rift. Whatever future they might still have together, she would place in Pax's hands. She only hoped he would take care of it the same way she would.

As Emma continued to work—and keep a close eye on the front of the house for Pax's departure—the sun beat down with all the ruthlessness of a steamy August day. She was going to be a sweat-stained, smelly guttersnipe by the time she was able to talk to him. In an effort to ease the heat some, she wound her hair up on top of her head and cinched it there with a hair tie she'd put in her skirt pocket that morning. Her soaking-wet T-shirt clung to her torso, so she stripped down to the tank top she was wearing underneath it, not caring that its scooped back revealed her telltale tattoo in all its glory. It was hot. She was irritable. No one was home except Haven and Bennett, who she was confident wouldn't know the significance of the mark. Pax would be seeing it by day's end anyway. Emma just couldn't find it in herself to care anymore. She was tired of having to pretend to be someone she wasn't. She was actually looking forward to coming clean to Pax as soon as she could.

She had finished tending to the landscaping and was

tugging the gloves from her hands when a car pulled up in front of Summerlight and parked behind Pax's. A car she didn't recognize. A car with license plates from someplace other than New York—though, from this distance, she couldn't identify where for sure. But when three young men emerged from the car and started looking around, Emma halted her movements, willing herself to be invisible. Because there was something about those three young men looking around that set off sirens in every corner of her brain.

They were just tourists, she tried to tell herself. Pax must have posted some new photos or info about Summerlight on some of its social media accounts. Every time that happened, the mansion received a handful of visits from some of its fans who were "in the area" or "just passing through" and wanted to take a look at the place they'd been following up close and personal. Haven had told Emma that last year, before Christmas, Pax had started a movement on a popular crowdfunding site, to help her save the mansion that Bennett, at that time, had wanted to tear down. The appeal had gone viral, and Haven had raised a huge pile of cash that was allowing them to completely rehab the place. Since then, Summerlight itself had become something of a celebrity among DIY and old-house enthusiasts, and it had regularly spawned a handful of visitors here and there.

These three young men must be such enthusiasts, she tried to tell herself. Even though the couple of times other people had stopped by since she'd been here, they'd been retired couples or families or girls' retreat types. Not once had she known three young men to be interested in a place like Summerlight.

Unfortunately, she had seen a lot of men like that interested in Amber Finch.

Impossible, she told herself. There was no way they could know she was here.

As if cued by the thought, one of the men looked her way. When he saw her, he smiled a very ugly smile and batted at the man next to him. Who then batted at the third man, next to him. When all three were looking at her, she knew that it was indeed possible. Because the way they were looking at her and the way they muttered to each other under their breath and the way their smiles mimicked the smiles of so many other proud Swope fans who had spotted her, she knew. She knew even better when they quickly—and menacingly—started walking her way. She knew they knew she was Amber Finch. And she knew they weren't going to be satisfied until they had Amber Finch tied to their bumper like a hunting trophy and were driving off into the sunset.

She looked around for her shirt and realized it was hanging on a bush far behind her. She couldn't turn around to grab it, because they would see her tattoo, so she began to walk backward in that direction. Within three steps, she tripped over a stray branch she'd pruned and fell onto her fanny. The vulnerable position just made the men hasten their stride. So she rose quickly and started to back up again. But they immediately fanned out in front of her so that any way she turned to run, one of them would catch her before she got far. She kept her back firmly out of their view and continued to carefully pick her way in reverse. Not that they were even looking at her back—yet—because they were all focused so intently on her face.

"Yeah, that's her," the first one said.

The others nodded.

"Hello there, Amber Finch," the second one said.

"We've been looking for you," the third chimed in.

Emma could hear voices on the patio behind her, Haven's and Pax's, and continued to back up toward them. She grabbed her shirt from the bush as she passed it and began to untangle it so she could put it back on. In her agitated state, however, she had trouble distinguishing sleeve opening from neck opening and couldn't quite position the garment the way she needed to to put it on.

As she strove to work it out, she somehow found her voice and told the men, "I'm sorry, but you have me mistaken for someone else. My name is Emma Brown."

One more step backward. Then two. Then three. All steps that the men covered, too. And still she couldn't free her shirt enough to put it on. She could hear Haven and Pax clearly now, but their conversation seemed to be winding down. Which meant they would be going back into the house any minute.

"Nice try, Amber," the first one told her. "But you can't hide now. We've got you on video. I mean, you look a lot different now than you did before, but Dino here—" he gestured toward the second man "—he designed a facial-recognition program a few months ago that could peg you even without all the makeup."

That's impossible, Emma thought. Not the part about the facial recognition, since a designer who knew what they were doing could have refined the existing software or created a new program to ID her that way. But any video taken of her early on by Swope's followers, back when they recognized her on the street and set their phones to record, had all been filmed on the West Coast. Even if they'd managed to ID her in profile or behind her hand, there was nothing online that could have possibly tied her to Summerlight. There was no way these guys could have located her here.

She remembered then that Pax had filmed her a couple of times at Summerlight, including a shot of her full face from the front, but she'd made him promise not to post any video of her online. As far as she knew, he'd been true to his word and hadn't. Last Emma had checked—which, admittedly, had been a couple of weeks ago—there was nothing on any of the inn's accounts that included her. No videos, no photos, nothing. And as angry with her as he had been the last time they met, she just couldn't see him posting any in retaliation. So how had these guys pinned her location to here?

"Travis is gonna be *soooo* happy when we bring you in," the second man said. "You and he are gonna have a lot of fun together."

The third man grinned lasciviously. "And we're gonna have fun with you, too."

Her stomach rolled again as they began to describe, in graphic detail, all the ways they would "have fun" with her. She told herself to call out to Pax and Haven for help. She tried to call out to Pax and Haven for help. But somehow her voice got caught in her throat. It only made it worse when the men began to draw closer. As much as she'd always thought she would flee when this situation came up again—because somehow she had always known this situation would come up again—she froze instead. She couldn't even make her hands move to untangle her shirt.

And still the three men kept coming.

"Okay, so that's a yes on the garden video," Pax said as he and Haven concluded their meeting, "and a no on the boathouse video."

She nodded. "Yeah, the garden is gonna be hugely popular with people, but not that many are going to be interested in a boathouse renovation when the time comes. Especially since we don't even have a boat yet."

"But that leaves me down a video," Pax said. "I promised our Insta followers there would be two new clips up next week. I was going to do the garden prepping for fall and some 'before' shots of the boathouse. Now I got nothing for the second one."

He'd been extra busy with Summerlight's social media over the past two weeks, since he was pretty much prepped for the new semester and was still waiting to hear back on a couple of other projects. And also because he'd needed something to keep his brain busy so it wouldn't keep dwelling on thoughts about Emma. And memories of Emma. And that one incredible night he'd spent with Emma.

Or whoever the hell she was, since her name wasn't Emma.

His brain had also spent way too much time replaying his last conversation with her. The one he'd been so certain put everything about her into perspective and proved just what a liar and villain she was. She must be a villain. Because she was definitely a liar. And the reasons people lied were always villainous in nature. Either they wanted to take advantage of someone, or they wanted to hide something horrible about who they were.

Always.

Instead, replaying that last conversation between them had only made Pax feel more restless. More confused. More contrite. Like maybe he'd overreacted. Like maybe he should have cut her a little slack. Like maybe he should have put at least a little credence into what she'd told him, even if it did sound like a big, fat lie.

Like there might be some reasons people lied that weren't villainous.

"Maybe you could do one on the kitchen," Haven suggested in response to his concern about being short a video. "People who cook love looking at other people's kitchens. And Summerlight still has its original appliances, even if we're going to use the new ones after we open. You could film Emma making her famous grilled-cheese sandwiches on that monstrous old stove. It'd be great."

Aaaand there she was again, invading his thoughts. Though she had looked pretty cute, he recalled, making dinner for them at a century-old stove that was the size of a compact car. It really would make for a fun video. If it weren't for the fact that he had no intention of ever speaking to her again. And if it weren't for the fact that she'd forbidden him to film her.

"Maybe," he told Haven. "I'll see what kind of spin I can put on it. It could work."

Not that he would film Emma at the stove, since that was off-limits. And also because he wasn't speaking to her. But Haven was right—a lot of people loved kitchens.

The two of them finished up, then Haven headed back into the house. Pax said his goodbyes to her then and there, because he wanted to make one more sweep of the inn and its grounds before he went back to Ithaca, to see if any other ideas came to him.

He stepped off the patio and rounded the corner of the mansion to find Emma facing off with a trio of men he'd never seen before. A trio of men who looked in no way friendly. A trio of men who were moving toward her in a way that could only be called predatory. Emma was frozen to the spot, not speaking, not moving. But what caught Pax's attention the most in that instant was the tattoo spanning her upper back, from one shoulder blade to the other.

The fact that she had a tattoo on her back didn't surprise him, since he'd noticed in that one photo he had of her that she did have part of one peeking out from the top of her shirt. What did surprise him was that he recognized the tattoo. Anyone who'd spent any amount of time on the internet over the past year would recognize it. It had been plastered everywhere last fall, especially in online forums that attracted a certain…ilk. Even as recently as two weeks ago, when he'd gone deeper into the web to look more into Emma's deception after realizing her online photos had been photoshopped, Pax had seen that tattoo pop up in a number of places.

It was pretty much the brand of one of the most notorious enemies of the manosphere. In particular, the followers—or maybe he should say cult members—of an equally notorious, and self-proclaimed, "men's lifestyle expert." Travis Swope. Possibly the most odious, ridiculous, pathetic excuse for a human being to ever walk the planet. One who had been absolutely humiliated a year ago by some unknown upstart who came out of nowhere and challenged him on his own turf after he posted an especially hateful critique of strong, independent women. Litha Firefly, she'd called herself on that occasion. Though, later, she had been outed by Swope's hangers-on as a makeup vlogger named Amber Finch.

And wow, had Amber Finch made Travis Swope look like an absolute moron. Most people, Pax included, thought she was kind of an internet hero. She'd kicked the throne right out from under Swope, and he had yet to recover. He'd posted so many retaliatory takedowns of women in general and Amber in particular, none of which had come close to the rapier wit and seething sarcasm that Amber had hurled at him. Every time he tried to defend himself and put her down, he just sounded that much more stupid. It didn't help that, for a while there at the beginning, she'd kept swooping in whenever he posted a new attack on her to take him down yet another peg. And beautifully, at that.

No, her efforts hadn't shut him up, but he'd certainly been neutered to a very large degree. Last time Pax checked, his followers had numbered about half what they did at his peak. His sponsors and advertisers—who were pretty much as awful as he was—had left in droves. Anyone with a working brain had been forced to view the guy in a new light—which was as dim a bulb as Swope was himself. For the past year, he'd been throwing hissy fits and tantrums to rival the whiniest toddler.

In an effort to finally shut her up last year, he'd sent his flying monkeys after her to the tune of a six-figure bounty, and they'd gone looking for her. Pax hadn't really followed the drama that closely, but he'd read enough to know the poor woman had been doxed and forced to flee her home, and everyone who still followed Swope—and a bunch who didn't follow him but could use a big payload—had started looking for her. A *lot* of people had wanted a piece of Amber Finch. A *lot* had wanted to find her. But no one ever had.

Until now. Not just Pax, but these guys surrounding her obviously knew who she was, too, because their language was… Oof. The vocabulary of the very, very stupid and crass. And now Pax understood why Emma had lied to him for months. She'd tried to tell him two weeks ago, he now realized. She'd confessed as much as she could to him without revealing who she was. But why hadn't she trusted him enough by then to tell him everything?

Oh, right. Because he'd been an absolute dick that day, so certain there could be no legitimate reason for lying that he hadn't considered a word she said as honest. No wonder she hadn't wanted to tell him the truth.

He'd been behaving just like the scumbags who had been making her life miserable.

His understanding grew as he neared Emma and the group of men approaching her. She took a few uncertain steps backward, toward Pax, and he heard her insist that her name was Emma Brown. Truly, she added as she dragged her shirt over her head to hide her tattoo, she had no idea who this Amber Finch person was that they were looking for. Evidently these guys hadn't seen her tattoo yet, and she wanted to keep it that way. She looked at each man individually, then to her left and right, as if she were planning her moves like an NFL running back. Pax wouldn't have been surprised if she did just that. She'd obviously been protecting herself for the better part of a year, doing whatever she'd had to do to keep herself safe from an angry mob. Breaking through these guys would be a piece of cake.

He strode forward as she continued to move back, with the three guys following. They were so focused on her, they hadn't noticed his presence yet, and as the group drew nearer to him, he could clearly hear what they were telling her. And what he heard made his flesh crawl. Because the things they were going to do to her, which they described in vivid detail, were things that made his stomach pitch. Things Swope would do to her, too, once they were done with her. It was all Pax could do not to push his way past her and beat the ever-loving crap out of every one of them.

Instead he cheerfully called out "Emma!" as he completed the last few steps it took to pull up behind her, injecting a nonchalance into his voice he was nowhere close to feeling.

The three men finally looked at him after that—seriously, how dumb did you have to be to not even notice someone crashing your scumbag party?—and immediately stopped talking. *Yeah, you'll gang up on a five-foot-four woman who weighs half as much as you do, but when a guy your size enters the conversation, you shut up like the big crybabies you are.* Had Pax thought he was angry before? 'Cause he was starting to seethe now. Dumbasses.

"There you are, sweetheart," he added as he came up beside her and looped an arm affectionately around her waist. "I've been looking all over for you."

She turned at his approach, the terror so evident in her expression mixing with clear relief at his appearance. Even though they'd parted badly the last time they were together, it was obvious neither of them was thinking about that right now. They had a lot to talk about later. But first things first.

He pulled her close and dropped a quick kiss on the crown of her head. She leaned into him as if they'd never spoken a cross word to each other in their lives, roping both arms around his waist. He could feel her trembling against him, and his anger grew even more.

Still looking at Emma, he asked, "Who are your new friends?"

She shook her head. "They're not my friends. They think I'm someone I'm not. And they're saying some very mean things."

Pax gaped at her in a way that would be comical were

it not for the severity of the situation. Then he turned that gape onto the three men as if he were their maiden great-aunts chastising them: *Goodness gracious, how impolite—your mothers would be so disappointed.*

"Maybe I can help, snookums," he said to Emma, his voice dripping with honey. To the men, he said, "Is there a problem, gentlemen?"

The three exchanged concerned looks, then turned their attention back to Pax. They suddenly looked nowhere near as confident as they had when they were verbally attacking Emma. Dumbasses.

Finally the one in the center spoke. "We got no beef with you, dude. We just want the girl."

Pax did his best to look benignly curious. "What girl?"

The three exchanged glances again, then looked back at Pax. One of the other apes nodded at Emma.

"That girl?"

Just to mess with them, Pax turned and looked behind himself and Emma, then back at the three men. "I don't see any girls here. You guys might need to see an ophthalmologist. That's an eye doctor," he added helpfully, since that was a really big word for guys like them.

They continued to scowl at him, but they made no move to challenge him the way they had Emma. One of the dumbasses pointed at Emma again. "That girl," he said. "The one right beside you."

Now Pax looked at Emma. "Oh, her," he said. "Yeah, she's not a girl. She's a woman."

"Whatever," said the third dumbass. "Just turn around

and go back to doing whatever you were doing. She's coming with us."

Pax put on his naive face again. "Why would she be coming with you? She said she doesn't even know you."

"Maybe not," the first dumbass said. "But we know her."

"And how do you know my fiancée, Emma Brown? Are you guys from Altoona, too?"

Beside him, Emma's trembling eased a little, but the arms around his waist wrenched tighter.

"What are you talking about?" the middle cretin said. "She's Amber Finch. You know who that is?"

Pax nodded. "I do. She's awesome. I nearly split a gut laughing at how she showed Travis Swope—and anyone else with access to the internet—what an absolute tool he is. Did you guys see that? Did you not love it? That guy is *such* a jackass."

Clearly they had not loved it. Clearly they did not consider Travis Swope to be a tool or jackass. Pax didn't care. "Anyway, I don't know what makes you think my fiancée, Emma Brown, is Amber Finch, but she's not." He lifted a hand in farewell. "Happy trails."

"She's totally Amber Finch," dimwit number one said. "Maybe she's calling herself Emma Brown now, but we saw her in a video about this place that's been making the rounds. Ran some facial-recognition app on her and Amber Finch, and it came back a match."

Pax knew a moment of unqualified dread. Emma had told him, emphatically, not to post any videos for the inn that had her in them. And he hadn't. Well, not any videos that had her as the central feature. But there had been one or two shots with her in the background, far enough removed or in bad enough light that it shouldn't have been a problem. He was reasonably sure no one could have ID'd her through facial-recognition software in any of those shots.

Then he remembered he hadn't really been paying much attention to what he'd posted about the inn in the last two weeks. He'd just been trying to keep his head filled with anything that didn't include memories of how much he'd come to love Emma and how much he'd been betrayed by Emma. He'd slapped up some hastily edited footage, and a couple of times he hadn't even bothered to edit the shots he uploaded, thinking they were fine the last time he looked at them.

Obviously, those shots hadn't been fine. At least when it came to ensuring he kept his promise to Emma.

Because, he realized now, he hadn't really taken her concerns about potentially being endangered by other people seriously. He'd just thought she was being dramatic and kind of ridiculous about it. But she'd known something like this could happen. She'd known it would put her at risk. By being so careless, Pax had…

Well. He'd just handed her over to the torch-bearing mob that had been looking for her for almost a year.

Chapter Thirteen

Somehow he managed to keep his composure in light of this discovery and not give away the panic coursing through him inside. Probably because this was what he'd been brought up to do—pretend to be and do and feel things he wasn't and didn't. He'd learned well when he was young how to mask truth and reality. How to make people believe things that were in no way true. He could sell a con under any circumstances. Even this one. Especially this one. Because Emma's safety depended on it.

"There's no way this woman is Amber Finch," he assured the nitwits. "I've known her since the day she was born. Our parents were best friends. Hell, our grandparents were best friends. We were in school together from kindergarten to senior year."

All three morons exchanged wary glances, then turned back to Pax. "You're lying. She's Amber Finch."

"She's not Amber Finch," he insisted. "She's Emma Brown. We grew up together in Altoona." When one of the other creeps opened his mouth to object again, Pax continued. "That's in Pennsylvania. Home of Hedda Hopper and the original horseshoe curve, birthplace of Georgism and sister city to St. Pölten, Austria. It's a cool place. You should visit sometime. If you haven't already, I mean. 'Cause who wouldn't want to see the original horseshoe curve?"

The three goons were looking at Pax as if he'd just grown a third eye. He didn't care. He was just getting warmed up.

"She's Amber Finch," one of the other clowns said. "We've been looking for her."

"Well, you'll just have to look somewhere else," Pax told them. "Because there is no Amber Finch here. Only me and my Emma."

At this, he gave her a quick hug.

The men exchanged glances again, then the first one said, "Prove it."

Well, if he insisted.

At this, Pax cracked his mental knuckles and entered into that realm he'd ruled so effortlessly as a kid but had turned his back on for more than a decade. The ease with which he slipped back into being the ultimate con artist probably should have concerned him. And maybe it would later. For now, he had a part to play. And as he had so many times when he was young, he played it to the hilt.

He told the three dirtbags how he couldn't remember a time when he and Emma hadn't been joined at the hip, how much better she was than him at science, but how he always kicked her ass in Mathletes. He waxed rhapsodic about her prom dress, how the sapphire sequins had caught the light of the disco ball so beautifully and been so perfect for the theme of On Cloud Nine. He also told them how she was homecoming queen for their sophomore, junior *and* senior year, much to the irritation of Mandy Digby, who had been so sure it would be her, every single time. Damn, Mandy got so mad. Oh, and had they heard about how Emma took home the blue ribbon at the Pennsylvania State Fair for her Pfeffernüsse cookies? True story.

On and on he went, impressing even himself with the absolute tripe he was able to pull out of thin air. For the pièce de résistance, he finished his tale with the declaration, "And this time next year, lads, Emma and I are going to be married. Aren't we, smoochykins?"

He had felt her relax as he was weaving his tale of their epic romance until she was holding him the way she used to, when the two of them had been on better terms. At his announcement of their wedding, she nodded in eager agreement. But since she said nothing to elaborate, he wasn't sure if her frame of mind was as calm as her posture. So Pax continued to do the talking for both of them.

"Yep, we're getting married right here at Summerlight." He pointed toward the garden. "In that very garden. Fifty guests, can you imagine? I think they'll all fit, though. I just hope my uncle Augie doesn't try to pull one of his notorious wedding pranks. Like when he chained a bowling ball to my cousin Chip's ankle that was stenciled with his new bride Cookie's name. And before you can say it," he added, lifting a hand, palm out, "I know. Chip and Cookie. Believe me, the whole family has a laugh every time we get together for the holidays."

A long moment passed when all three of the scum-bags exchanged glances again, as if they were all trying to figure out what the hell had just happened. Always a good sign when running a con if the mark ended up looking like someone just smacked on the back of their head with a two-by-four. Pax silently wished them luck figuring it all out.

Nah, just kidding. What he was wishing them, they didn't want to know.

Finally, dumbass number one—the king dumbass, evidently—told Pax, "If she's not really Amber Finch, if she's this Emma Brown you say she is, then she can prove it by showing us her back."

Beside him, Emma stiffened again.

Pax made a face. "Why would she do something like that?"

"Because Amber Finch has a really identifiable tat-too. If your girlfriend here—"

"Fiancée," Pax corrected him.

"Whatever. If she's not Amber Finch, she won't have that tattoo."

Pax shook his head at them as if they were a bunch of three-year-olds who'd just asked for the latest in-demand, out-of-stock toy. "Sorry, guys—no can do," he told them. "There is no way my honeybun here is going to show you her back. Hell, *I* haven't even seen her back."

There went the exchange of curious looks again.

"But you said you're getting married," the middle goon said.

"Oh, we are," Pax assured them.

"But you've never seen her back?"

Pax shook his head.

"Why not?"

"Because it would be improper. We're Puritans."

Strangely, they didn't look like they believed him about that, either. So Pax launched into *another* extremely convincing, if he did say so himself, story about how their two families were direct descendants of Jonathan Edwards and Sarah Pierrepont—which, considering the fact that the two of them had had eleven children a few hundred years ago was actually not outside the realm of possibility—and how his and Emma's forebears had kept alive all the teachings of the Great Awakening, and by the way, did these three guys even know that much about the Great Awakening? Well, let Pax tell them all about it, because, frankly, after some of the things he'd just heard them say to his fiancée, they could use some old-time religion in their lives.

And then he did tell them all about the Great Awakening, because by then, they were hanging on his every word.

"Anyway," he said as he wound down, before they had a chance to think about just how unlikely it was that he and Emma, or anyone else for that matter, was a Puritan in this day and age—not that he thought for a moment that any of these guys thought too much about anything. "You should see the cake we ordered for the wedding. Emma here just insisted it had to be heart shaped, with *three* tiers, and she wanted these columns made out of plastic cupids to hold up each one of them—which, frankly, I could barf, but what am I gonna do? I love this woman. I'll do anything for her."

Even lie through my teeth without a care in the world.

For a long time, the three men only looked at him, then Emma, then back at him. Pax keep his expression bland as he held his breath, waiting to see if they would buy what just felt like the longest con he'd ever run. Finally, they all looked at each other again. Then they turned back and looked at the happy, soon-to-be-wed Puritan couple.

"You are such a simp," the first dimwit told Pax.

"Livin' in a gynocracy," the second moron said.

"Totally PW'd," the third idiot agreed.

Pax just smiled. "Someday, if you guys are lucky enough to fall in love the way I have, you'll understand." But since chances were good that none of them were ever even going to get laid, he wasn't going to hold his breath.

Instead, he dropped a kiss onto the top of Emma's head again, then, with much reluctance, released her. Then he tucked her behind his back and put on the most menacing face he could conjure. It was a good one, too. One he used to use a lot when he was still a part of the family. One that had scared the crap out of anyone—anyone—who ever challenged him. Marks, cops, other members of the family…anyone.

"Now then, gents," he said in the even, borderline-sociopathic voice he used to use to accompany the expression. "I think you need to be leaving. You've said more than enough to the woman I'm planning to spend the rest of my life with. And I think it's time for you to go."

He took a few slow, deliberate steps forward as he

spoke, erasing the distance between himself and the three amigos as he went. The closer he drew to them, the more they retreated. Again, it struck him how easy it was for people to prey on those who were physically weaker or outnumbered by them. It reminded him—too much—of the family he'd left behind. Involuntarily, his hands curled into fists.

And in his chilling, threatening voice, he told them, "Have a nice day."

The three men turned around, grumbling as they picked their way across the yard about how they had been so sure they would find Amber Finch here and how much their stupid mistake had cost them in gas and burgers and wondering if maybe Travis Swope would pay them back, because they'd been so sure they would be successful.

Yeah, right, Pax thought. *Bill the guy and see what happens.*

Damn, he still had it. He'd even sold the whole Puritan thing. How the hell had those guys actually bought that? Oh, right. Not the sharpest knives in the drawer to begin with. All that mattered was that he had convinced them they were wrong about Emma. They wouldn't be coming back or spreading around online that Amber Finch had been spotted in the Finger Lakes, thanks to the heap of lies he'd just told them. Obviously there were times when a person had a very good reason for lying. Obviously telling a lie—or a whole pile of them—didn't necessarily make someone a bad person. It just depended on the situation. And the reason. And the person.

He watched as the three morons started their car and made a three-point-turn that came *this* close to knocking down Summerlight's mailbox—wow, they really were idiots—as they drove off toward the main road. Then he turned around to look at Emma. Amber. He wondered what she wanted to go by now.

"I am so sorry these guys found you," he told her. "I must have inadvertently uploaded some video onto one of the Summerlight accounts that included you. It wasn't on purpose, Emma—I swear. My head just hasn't been in a good place for the last couple of weeks, and I haven't really been giving my full attention to the things I should be giving it to, and I must have just..." He expelled a rough sigh. "I led them right to you. I'm sorry."

"I believe you," she said. Without hesitation, too, a consideration he certainly hadn't afforded her two weeks ago. "And honestly if it hadn't been you doing that, it would have been something else. Especially once the inn opens. There are going to be tons of people here. I'm going to be recognized again eventually. This was just a reminder for me not to get too complacent."

She looked at the place where the three men had stood only moments ago, and a shudder went through her body that was so bad, Pax could actually see it. He crossed the distance that separated them and pulled her into his arms again. She was still trembling. That was how badly those pieces of crap had shaken her. He couldn't believe how close he had come to putting her in irrevocable danger.

"I'm sorry," he said again. "You tried to tell me two weeks ago, didn't you?"

She nodded. "I wanted to be honest with you. But the way you were acting that day, I just... I couldn't. I know you were hurt, Pax," she hurried to add. "I know I did that, and I'm sorry, too. But I just... I couldn't tell you the truth then. I'm sorry."

"You don't have anything to apologize for," he told her. "I remember when the whole Travis Swope–Amber Finch thing went down. I remember what some of those jerks said they would do to you if they ever got their hands on you."

And he remembered, too, hearing about all the times Amber Finch had been spotted in the wild and how close some of those guys had come to grabbing her for Swope. Some literally had grabbed her, he'd read—had actually put hands on her and tried to force her into a van, only to have her escape. There had been other such stories, other such threats. He couldn't imagine what it must have been like to have people you didn't even know attacking you. Figuratively and literally.

She nodded wearily. "Yeah, well, anything you read was tame compared to what they said to me in messages and emails and texts once I was outed as Amber Finch. Even these guys couldn't hold a candle to some of them."

She hadn't quite stopped shaking, and she had both arms wrapped around him again, as if he was all that was keeping her from crumbling to the ground.

"Are you okay?" he asked her.

She nodded. Another lie—she wasn't okay. But Pax didn't react to the gesture the way he used to react when someone lied to him. Saying she was okay after something like what had just happened to her wasn't an act of dishonesty. It was an act of courage. He had a feeling she'd had to tell herself she was okay a lot since she went on the run, even when she knew she wasn't. It was probably the only way she'd been able to make it through the day.

"It's just been a rough year, you know?" she said.

A year, Pax marveled. He remembered the fall semester had just started, and Amber Finch was all the talk in some of his computer-science classes. Mostly from dumbass guys who were so sure Amber Finch deserved whatever she got, and wouldn't it be nice to find her and collect the reward? But not until after they'd had a go at her first.

His anger returned when he remembered some of the vulgar, hateful threats he'd heard from some of the male students—spoken so blatantly and carelessly in front of the handful of women students in his classroom—before he'd shut them up and threatened them himself with write-ups to the dean of admissions, suggesting their admissions be revoked. He could only imagine some of the things Emma… *Amber*, he corrected himself…had heard directed at her personally. For almost a year.

"You want to talk about it?" he asked.

"Not really," she told him. Honestly this time. "Not in detail. Not yet. But I do want you to know where I was coming from when I wasn't honest with you."

He held up a hand before she even finished talking. "You don't have to do that," he said. "I can imagine."

"No, you can't," she said emphatically. "You can't

possibly imagine some of the things guys have said
to me and threatened to do to me over the last year—
in email, in texts, in phone calls and in person. And
you will never be able to appreciate how terrifying it
is to realize you'd be absolutely helpless to stop them
if they ever found you and got their hands on you and
did those things."

He wondered just how many times Amber Finch
had been approached the way Emma had today. Even
once was one too many. But Emma told him about a
lot more than one. And every episode left him feeling
sicker than the one before it.

"I barely escaped a couple of times," she told him.
"I don't even want to think about what would have
happened on those times—what would have happened
today—if they'd actually caught me. But I dreamed
about it. A lot. Even sleeping didn't ease the fear."

Pax knew he shouldn't be surprised by the awful,
awful things one person could say and do to another.
Hell, he lived on the internet, where people said and
did awful things all the time. Usually under the protec-
tion of being anonymous, but sometimes just flat-out
declaring proudly that they would take joy in making
anyone who wasn't like them suffer in the most heinous ways possible. Hell, Pax had spent the better part
of his teen years on the dark web among other criminals and reprobates, and he'd heard even worse things
said there. There truly was no limit to the evilness and
ugliness some human beings could embrace.

But even having been exposed to all that, the things

Emma—Amber, he corrected himself again—told him made his flesh crawl.

"They would have done it, too," she said. "Without a single qualm. That's how bad an influence Travis Swope is on these guys. And there are other Travis Swopes out there, all over the internet. Women are becoming prey in this country—on this entire planet—like they've never been preyed upon before. It is so scary just being a woman sometimes."

He tried to imagine what it must be like for her and other women like her, but she was right. He was at the top of the food chain when it came to the dregs of the internet—he was male, cisgender, heterosexual, and white. On first glance, Travis Swope's followers would consider Pax one of them, as much as he hated to realize it. And they would leave him alone. He had no idea what it was like to be the target of, well, anything. And he was big enough and fit enough that, in most situations, he could take care of himself. Emma was half the size of a lot of these guys. She'd be overpowered in no time by even one of them. It was no wonder she'd been living the way she had. If he'd been in her position, he would have done the same thing. He would have begged, borrowed or stolen, and he would have lied his heart out to survive.

"I really did want to be honest with you," she said. "As much as I could be. And really, I never lied to you beyond my name. Maybe I wasn't completely honest with you, and maybe I kept myself from having to lie through creative punctuation or by changing the subject, but…"

"I'm sorry I called you a liar," he said. "And I'm sorry I didn't listen when you tried to explain. The way I was brought up, people only lied for one reason—to hurt other people. I didn't think there was anything you could say that would change my mind about that."

"I would never hurt you," she told him. "Not on purpose."

"I know that."

She smiled. A small smile, but it was more genuine than a lot of the ones he'd seen from her. "Besides, in some ways, I was kind of a liar."

He shook his head. "Liars lie to take advantage of people. You were doing what you had to do to survive."

"I was honest with you when it came to all the important stuff," she told him. "Maybe I didn't do all the things Emma Brown from Altoona did, but all the things I told you about me personally, the things I like and don't like, the things I believe, the things I know— all of that was me, not her. And when I told you I loved you…" Here, her eyes grew damp. "Pax, I'd never been more honest about anything in my life."

He noticed how when she told him she *loved* him, she used the past tense. He hoped it was only because it was a figure of speech and not, you know, the truth and that she no longer loved him. Not that he really deserved her love after the way he'd behaved and after some of the things he'd said to her. If he had to earn her love all over again, he'd do whatever he had to do. Because nothing in his life had ever been sweeter than being loved by Emma Brown. Amber Finch, he meant. Oh, hell, he didn't care what her name was. Only who she was. And to him, she was the person he wanted to spend the rest of his life with.

Just to be sure, he asked, "You loved me? As in past tense? You don't anymore?"

Her eyes widened. "Oh, God, no."

Pax started to panic.

"I mean yes," she hurried to clarify. "Yes, I still love you. I'll always love you."

Okay, then. He knew he still had a lot to make up for. But at least he knew where to start.

"I can't believe you lied for me," she said, smiling again. "I mean, you told some absolute whoppers. I don't think I've ever heard anyone lie the way you just did. And here I thought lying was the worst thing a person could do in your eyes."

He shook his head. "Maybe it was once, but now I know there's something even worse than lying."

She arched her brows in silent question.

"Turning your back on someone who loves you," he told her. "Someone you love, too. If keeping you safe means lying, Emma, I will lie like a dog."

She squeezed him tighter. "I can't believe how convincing you were. I mean, seriously, Puritans? Where did all that stuff about the Great Awakening come from?"

"Remember how I told you I spent a lot of time in the library when I was kid? I know a lot of things about a lot of things. Don't even think about being on an opposing team from me on trivia night. You only want to be with me."

She smiled. "That's true. I do only want to be with you."

He smiled back. "How convenient. I only want to be with you, too."

He bent his head to hers and kissed her, a soft, leisurely kiss of both apology and promise. A promise to be faithful and true, in whatever form that took. As long as they were honest with their feelings and true to each other, that was all that really mattered. When they pulled apart, Emma inhaled a deep breath and released it slowly, her body easing as if she were literally unshouldering all the bad things that had happened to her over the past year.

"I'm sorry you had to live the way you've had to live for so long," he said softly.

Instead of looking sad, she smiled again. "I'm kind of not. As bad as it was, it brought me here, and I found you. Weirdly, I guess I have Travis Swope to thank for both the worst and best things that have ever happened to me."

"That doesn't mean we have to invite him to the wedding, does it?"

Though Pax did spare a moment to think about that and how great it would be to rub the guy's nose in it that what he had planned to be a living hell for Amber Finch actually ended up being her happily-ever-after. That was probably the biggest, most annoying takedown of him she could make.

Emma looked up at his remark. Very softly, she asked, "What wedding?"

Pax lifted a shoulder and let it drop. But all he said was "We have a lot to talk about."

She nodded. "Yeah, we do. I just wish this whole

sorry chapter of my life was truly over so I could move into a new one. But guys like the ones today are going to keep coming after me as long as there's a price on my head."

"Maybe," Pax agreed. "But you don't have to do this alone anymore. I've got your back."

What little tension left in her body seemed to completely ease at his assurance. Tears came to her eyes again, but she fiercely swiped them away. All she said, very softly, was "Thanks."

Then she looped both arms around his waist again and squeezed tight. Pax returned the embrace, pulling her as close to himself as he could. For a long time, she only leaned into him, and little by little, her trembling subsided completely. Even then, though, she didn't let him go. So he held on to her, too, until she was ready to release him. After several more long moments, she finally loosened her hold a bit. But she still didn't let go, even when she pulled away enough to look at him.

"This feels really good," she said. "I forgot how nice it is to even just hug someone. You're right—I've been living this way, all alone, for too long. Thank you for being here, Pax."

"I'll be here as long as you want me, Emma." He hesitated. "Or should I call you Amber now?"

She expelled a sound that was a mix of resolution and uncertainty. "I don't know," she finally told him. "I don't feel like Amber Finch anymore. I haven't felt like her for a long time. I'm not sure I even really knew her that well. But I'm not Emma Brown, either. Not the one from Altoona anyway. I need to give her back her identity."

"So if you're not Amber Finch and you're not Emma Brown," he echoed, "then who are you going to be?"

She thought for a moment. "I don't know. Maybe a mix of both. Amber's experiences over the last year have certainly made her more thoughtful and compassionate than she used to be, but she's not the low-key, simple-life, small-town girl that Emma Brown is, either." She looked at Pax. "I guess I've kind of blended them both together into a new person. And I have a feeling I'm not done yet. But who I'll be when it all plays out…"

She shrugged, too. "I'm not Amber Finch *or* Emma Brown. Guess I'm going to need a new name to go with my new identity. That would help keep the flying monkeys at bay, too."

"Maybe you could take a bit from each name," he said. "Become Amber Brown or Emma Finch. Or even…"

"What?"

Pax's heart began to race as he put the thought into words. "You could be Amber Lightfoot."

She didn't say anything for a couple of seconds. Or eons. Hard to tell when he was waiting for a reply to a proposal like that. Finally, though, she smiled. "You want me to take your last name?"

"If you want to."

"That's so old-fashioned."

"Yeah, well."

"Amber Lightfoot," she said. She smiled. "Yeah, that could work."

Pax grinned. Amber grinned.

"We have a lot to talk about," he said again.

She nodded. "Yeah, we do."

They shared one more lengthy, tender kiss, then turned to make their way to the patio. As they sat down on a bench facing the lake, they said nothing at first. He wasn't sure if they'd start talking right away or put it off for a bit. Honestly, he didn't care. He only wanted to be with the woman beside him, and he wanted to be with her forever, and he didn't care what they did or called each other in the meantime.

As if reading his mind, though, she said, "Smoochy-kins? Where did that come from?"

"What, you don't like smoochykins?" Pax asked. "You're a total smoochykins."

"I really don't think I'm a smoochykins. Or a honeybun," she added when she must have remembered that affront to endearments everywhere.

"All right," he said. "Then, how about if I call you pookie?"

She bit back a smile at that. But she told him, "No."

"Snookums?"

"No."

"Buttercup?"

"I am no one's buttercup."

"Doodle bug?"

Now she was laughing out loud. "Pax! Stop it!"

"Well, I have to call you something. We have a lot to talk about."

She sighed. "I don't know. I've been Emma for so long, and I kind of don't feel like Amber anymore."

Pax grinned. "Smoochykins it is, then."

She cuffed him playfully on the shoulder, wrapped her arms around his waist again and leaned in as if she had no intention of ever letting him go.

But as much as the two of them talked about that day, even when the sun was dipping toward the horizon and the moon was starting to rise, she never, not even once, told him he couldn't call her smoochykins.

Epilogue

Amber Lightfoot—yes, she did like her new name—
sat in her new desk chair in her new office in Ithaca
Commons and gave it an experimental twirl. Yep, it was
a good chair. Totally worth the fifty bucks she spent on
it at her and Pax's favorite thrift store. Thrifted, too,
was the rolltop desk, the pair of glass-covered librar-
ian bookcases and the Persian rug. So Pax liked retro?
Well, Amber would show him retro. She'd gone full-on
Victorian when it came to furnishing her new space.

She'd had no idea she liked stuff this old. She'd never
really thought about it. When she furnished her condo
in Seattle a million years ago, she'd just chosen what
she figured tech-oriented people always chose for their
homes. Clean lines, little decoration, minimalism up
the wazoo. But when she decided to go back into the
tech-security biz under her new, soon-to-be-married
name—it was what she did best, after all—and when it
came time to furnish the office space, she found herself
drawn, again and again, to old things. Even older than
what Pax liked. It had been eye-opening.

Her furniture preference wasn't the only new thing
Amber had discovered about herself in the six months

since Pax learned who she really was. She'd decided to keep her natural hair color, though it now bore a bright fuchsia streak on each side from roots to ends. She also still had a killer hand at eyeliner and lip contouring and so had embraced those again, but she'd decided cosmetics vlogging wasn't really her thing after all. And although she had ditched the earth-mother-goddess look, she hadn't gone back to her Goth Girl ways. Instead, she'd kind of incorporated both styles to give herself a look that was… Hmm. Pax called her style *eclectic*. To Amber, it was just, well, Amber Lightfoot style. Today she was wearing an oversize ivory sweater over a trendy houndstooth skirt, fishnets, and Doc Martens. A little bit of old, a little bit of new. Kind of like how her state-of-the-art MacBook Pro was sitting on a desk that had been around since before electricity even entered the average home.

As if conjured by her thoughts of him, Pax rapped lightly at her office door and pushed it open, poking his head inside. The spring semester had started a month ago, but that was belied by the fact that there was currently four inches of snow on the ground outside.

"Ready for lunch, smoochykins?" he asked.

As she always did whenever he called her by his pet name, she laughed.

"Past ready, snookums," she told him. Her stomach had been rumbling for the past hour.

Since it was Thursday, Pax was finished with his classes by noon, so they could enjoy the rest of the day together, working from home. Amber had continued with her position as housekeeper at Summerlight until just before Christmas, to help Haven and Bennett launch the place properly, but now there was a new housekeeper occupying the little room on the fourth floor that had been her sanctuary after months of living in fear.

Amber Lightfoot didn't live in fear. Last fall, Travis Swope's empire had come crumbling down around him when the feds came looking for him on charges of a host of unsavory felonies from drugs and pandering to money laundering and extortion. Last Amber had heard, Swope had barely had time to escape his Las Vegas party mansion with the clothes on his back and was now in hiding and on the run. Any six figures he might have had to pay out her bounty were now housed in frozen bank accounts the IRS was busy raiding.

In fact, he was the one with a bounty on his head now. His house was in foreclosure, and his cult of flying monkeys had scattered like rats. Except for the ones who were actively looking for him in the hopes of winning the reward from turning him in.

There was still enough of the old, snarky Amber inside her to like thinking about him eating out of a dumpster and sleeping under a bridge somewhere or scraping dried egg off a plate as he sweated in front of the Hobart in a diner kitchen. She hoped he had at least a good nine or ten months of living that way. Then she hoped the feds swooped in and locked him up for a good, long time.

Yeah, that's the ticket.

It wasn't the only thing in her and Pax's lives to have come full circle. Not only had Amber reconnected with

her West Coast friends, but last fall, at her encourage-
ment, Pax had messaged Mrs. Aebersold, the woman
he'd gone from scamming to treasuring, to both apologize again and see how she was doing. Instead of ignor-
ing or berating him, she'd messaged him back within
hours, delighted to know he had escaped the lifestyle to
which he was so ill suited and was doing well. They'd
stayed in close contact since, and now Pax and Amber
both had plans to visit her in Des Moines over spring
break. She would also be attending their wedding in
Summerlight's garden this summer.

In any event, the name Amber Finch was no longer
etched anywhere, digitally or literally, and the name
Emma Brown would not be appearing on her gravestone. Amber Lightfoot would not have to live her life
alone, darting from one place to another because she
was never safe. With Pax, she'd never felt safer in her
life. Not just her physical person, but her emotional
one, too. She knew he would always protect her, life
and limb, heart and soul. The same way she would always protect him in turn. They had each other's backs.

They had each other, period. And they would stay
that way forever.

* * * * *